THE COST
of PASSAGE

Crossings of Promise
Historical fiction with a touch of romance

Dianne Christner
Keeper of Hearts

Janice L. Dick
Calm Before the Storm
Eye of the Storm

Hugh Alan Smith
When Lightning Strikes
When the River Calls

Heather Tekavac
The Cost of Passage

THE COST
of PASSAGE

HEATHER TEKAVEC

Herald
Press

Waterloo, Ontario
Scottdale, Pennsylvania

National Library of Canada Cataloguing-in-Publication Data
Tekavec, Heather, 1969-
  The cost of passage / Heather Tekavec

(Crossings of promise)
ISBN 0-8361-9237-0

    I. Title. II. Series.

PS8589.E373C68 2004   C813'.6   C2004-901245-2

Scripture is from the King James Version.

THE COST OF PASSAGE
Copyright © 2004 by Herald Press, Waterloo, Ont. N2L 6H7.
    Published simultaneously in USA by Herald Press,
    Scottdale, Pa. 15683. All rights reserved
Canadiana Entry Number: C2004-901245-2
Library of Congress Control Number: 2004102199
International Standard Book Number: 0-8361-9237-0
Printed in the United States of America
Cover art by Barbara Kiwak
Cover design by Sans Serif Design Inc.

10 09 08 07 06 05 04 10 9 8 7 6 5 4 3 2 1

To order or request information, please call
1-800-759-4447 (individuals); 1-800-245-7894 (trade).
Website: www.heraldpress.com

*To my grandfather, Henry, who lived through
many of these events and always trusted God.
And to my grandmother, Susie, whose gift of storytelling
has always inspired me.*

Prologue

More than two hundred years ago, the Empress Catherine of Russia offered land to a group of people known as Mennonites. They were Christian people who loved the land and had a wonderful gift for farming it. Empress Catherine hoped that the Mennonites would settle the wild areas of Russia and be an example to her own people. In exchange, she offered them peace and promised that they would never have to fight in Russia's wars.

Years later, however, Empress Catherine died, and her promises died with her. Near the end of World War I, Russia started its own civil war. The two armies that battled for control of Russia were commonly known as the Red Army and the White Army. The Red Army were communists attempting to take over all of Russia, and the White Army fought to restore Russia to the rule of a czar. There was also a third group, sometimes called the Green Army, led by Nestor Makhno. The Green Army had its own rules and lived only to terrorize. Suddenly, there was no peace left. Not even for the Mennonites. . . .

Chapter 1

Anna and the Soldiers

Anna worked alongside her mother in uneasy silence. The distant rumble of airplanes came nearer and nearer, and the playful noise of the children outside had stopped. The only other sound was the deep gurgling in a pot on the hot, brick stove. Anna stared wearily up at the low kitchen ceiling, wishing for the hundredth time that day that this kitchen had a window.

Mama kept her eye on the two babies, ready to scoop them up at the first blast of bombing or gunfire. The rattling airplane engines grew louder and began to vibrate the pots hanging on the wall. Anna jumped as the front door banged open, echoing through the hall.

"Mama!" Anna's older brother, Peter, stumbled into the kitchen, nearly tripping over his muddy bootlaces in his haste. "White sheets, Ma!" he panted. His cheeks flamed as he huffed. "The soldiers outside . . . they need white sheets!"

Without question, Mama lifted her heavy skirts and swished past Peter. "Go get all the sheets from your room, Anna," Mama ordered as she raced off to her own bedroom. "Peter, watch the babies," she hollered over her shoulder.

Anna tossed her wooden spoon carelessly into the pot of boiling rhubarb, sending spatters of juice and bits of rhubarb flying in all directions. She pushed past Peter toward the children's bedroom and recklessly tore the crumpled white sheets off her brother's bed and the babies' cradle. When she reached the bed that she shared with eight-year-old Susie, she slowed down and carefully unfolded the corners, quickly peeking under the mattress to make sure her leather pouch was still hidden.

"Hurry up, hurry up," Peter urged impatiently from the hall until Anna appeared and shoved the rumpled sheets into his outstretched arms, with Mama's. Peter spun and raced back out to the busy street.

Anna dashed to the front window. The street was crowded with the rough, grimy soldiers who had recently moved into their village. The village children watched from the doors and windows of their houses, but Peter lingered on the edge of the street, as near the soldiers as he could be without getting hollered at by one of them.

"What's happening?" Mama asked from across the room. Her voice remained calm and steady, for the sake of the babies, but Anna could sense her worry in the way she hovered over them.

"It looks like the soldiers are trying to signal the planes. They're spreading your sheets on the ground." Anna knew that the thought of her sheets in the dirt would make Mama shudder almost as much as the planes overhead did.

"Are there many?"

Anna nodded, and a shiver shook her shoulders. It was a frightening sight, but an awesome one too. More warplanes than she had ever seen at once were circling and sweeping across their normally quiet sky.

"We should get into the cellar," Mama muttered, smoothing her apron the way she always did when she felt nervous. She scooped up the two small children, who were happily licking rhubarb bits off the wood floor. "Call Peter inside. And where is Susie?"

"Wait," Anna said suddenly. "I think the planes are leaving now. The soldiers are gathering your sheets." She leaped from the window to open the door and leaned out into the fresh spring breeze to catch the last glimpse of the planes as they flew into the distance. They weren't nearly as frightening when they flew away from the village.

The first time she had seen airplanes, only months ago, Anna guessed it was the most wonderful thing she would ever see—even better than the May Day Parade in Moscow's Red Square. Papa had taken her last year, for her thirteenth birthday. This year, they didn't go to Moscow though. It was no longer a safe place to visit. In fact, no place in Russia felt safe, and everyone, including Anna, had learned to fear the terrifying iron birds, which had recently been dropping bombs on other villages, not far away.

"I'll go get the sheets back," Anna volunteered, hurrying out before Mama could refuse her. She had been aching to get out of the hot kitchen all afternoon, but the work had never ended. The rhubarb had to be baked into pies, the garden vegetables needed to be canned, and the cream had to be churned into butter.

"Go quickly," Mama called after her. "Try to find Susie too. She is supposed to be working in the orchard, but I haven't seen a glimpse of her. And bring back some ham from the smoke room, please."

Anna wrinkled her nose, wishing she hadn't heard that part. To get to the smoke room, she had to go through the pig barn. She hated the pig barn. The smell made her stomach churn and twist.

Anna marched into the street, fanning herself as she breathed in the cooler air. Children slowly trickled back out to play in the new spring growth, and the armed soldiers stood proudly about, clapping each other on the back and gazing into the empty sky.

Peter glowed with the same pride as he carried their bundle of sheets back toward the house.

"What happened?" Anna asked him.

"Those planes were from the White Army," Peter told her with an air of importance. "But when they began circling, the soldiers down here feared that the pilots would mistake us for the Red Army."

"Us?" Anna questioned.

"I mean they—the White soldiers." Peter stumbled over his own words. "They thought the planes would bomb, thinking it was the Red Army down here, so they spread out white sheets as a signal that we—I mean—they were from the White Army too."

"You know you shouldn't be spending so much time around the soldiers," Anna scolded. "They're filthy, sinful monsters."

"Hush up or they'll hear you."

"So what if they do. They know they're not wanted here. Them or their dumb war."

"It isn't as though they're the Red Army," Peter retorted. "They're the good soldiers."

"There are no good soldiers," Anna hissed.

"I'll remember that when the Red's got you at gun point, and the White's aren't around to save you."

Anna grabbed the sheets from him and spun toward the smokehouse.

He was just impossible lately! When she complained to Mama about him, Mama said he was growing up and that's how fifteen-year-old boys act. Anna could see now that Mama might be right, at least partly. Peter did seem to be growing quickly. They used to be the same size, although Peter was a whole year older. And because they had the same nut-brown hair and freckled noses, people used to mistake them for twins. But nobody had made that mistake for a very long time. Peter now stood almost a head taller than she. He had a much deeper voice too and lumpy muscles where he used to have spindly arms like hers. But more than that had changed. He acted differently too. Ever since their "visitor" last month, he hadn't been the same.

∽

Anna remembered that night clearly. It had been a cool night and very quiet in their little house. They hadn't seen many soldiers in their small village since the fighting had begun, and they didn't expect to. Anna had been happily counting the coins in their freedom jar, while Susie set the table. Papa sat reading his Bible, and Peter lay sprawled on the floor in front of the crackling fire with three-year-old Henry and baby Elizabeth crawling all over him. The knock at their door had come with such force that Papa jumped to answer as if he were a child caught in mischief.

A soldier from the White Army stood there—or rather leaned there—against the doorpost. He looked exhausted, hollow-eyed, and frail. His torn uniform hung like a rag off his limp shoulders.

The soldier told them he had just escaped capture by the Red Army in a neighboring village. The babies had been afraid, and Mama gasped in horror, both at the sight of him and at the thought that the Red Army was so very near. But Papa humbly stepped aside and let him in. The White Army was not as ferocious as the Red. They didn't often hurt villagers or steal from them, but even if they had, Papa still would have seen only a needy man. The uniform didn't matter.

The soldier had stayed only a few hours. He ate most of Mama's special chicken stew and told Peter stories of bloody battles. "They're not human," he kept saying. "The Reds, they don't have no heart. I saw them take a man and . . ."

Anna plugged her ears against the vicious horror stories. She noticed Mama glare at him, then turn her back angrily and try to distract the little ones. Peter, however, listened wide-eyed.

The soldier kept talking. "But we'll get 'em," he promised. Anna didn't think he looked very convinced himself. "And when we do . . ." Again he began to fill their ears with gruesome accounts of revenge. Anna could see Peter's eyes lighting up and wished that Papa, as master of the house, would stop the talk, but even Papa, who wouldn't normally let such talk in his home, knew better than to rebuke such a hateful and vindictive man, who was trained to shoot his enemies.

Anna had to admit that the soldier had been friendly enough. Just a young kid forced into battle, as Papa said. Even Mama eventually relaxed enough to bandage his wounds. But when he left, he did something far worse than carrying a gun and talking of war. He did the one thing that Anna had feared since the war began. And for that one thing, she would never forgive him.

He asked for money.

The only money Papa could give him lay in the clay jar—the freedom jar—that Anna still clutched to ensure this soldier couldn't take it. The money had been carefully saved for sea passage to Canada, and it was as precious to them as pure water in drought. To Papa, going to Canada meant freedom to preach the word of God without fear of soldiers and a hateful government. To Mama it was passage to the land where she could walk outdoors in the winter and see flowers bloom in March, and never lose another child to a war she didn't believe in. Susie imagined that she would be an actress on stage in Canada, although Papa would never allow it. At least in Canada she could dream about it.

But Canada meant the most to Anna. Maybe it was because she understood the danger of staying in Russia better than the younger ones and was less attached to this foreign homeland than the older ones. Mostly though, it was because Canada had stolen her very best friend, Johnny, two years ago, and she wanted him back. She and Johnny had big dreams together in Canada. They planned to own their own candy factory and a whole chain of factories, right across the country. This had been their dream since they were eight years old, since the time when Johnny's wealthy uncle, Milton, had sent him creamy chocolate candy from his small factory in Canada. Johnny and Anna knew right from that moment that they wanted a chocolate factory too. Someday they would have all the chocolate they wanted. They would be rich then and extremely happy. Anna's mouth always watered when she thought about it.

"Your candy factory will make you fat before it makes you rich," Peter teased whenever she talked about it, but Anna didn't care. It was her dream—hers and Johnny's together. Besides, she was going to marry Johnny Warkentin someday, and he wouldn't care if she was fat.

And then Papa gave all that money to the soldier.

Anna hated soldiers, the way she believed every good Christian should. But Peter saw something different. Something Anna couldn't fathom. From that day on, he always tried to be near them. He cheered when they marched their disarmed prisoners through the streets, and he listened carefully to every static news brief on the small radio. He even watched out of the corner of his eye when the Red Army showed their hateful faces in town. He had never really been the same since that awful night.

❧

Now Anna stormed angrily toward the pig barn with sheets in hand, on her errand to get a ham from the smokehouse. The warm, damp smell of the fat pigs swirled around her as she got closer. Her stomach gurgled and her throat felt thick and sour. How could such smelly animals give such delicious ham? She could hear the pigs snorting in their pen, and she clapped her hand over her nose and mouth. She couldn't do it. She ran back to the front of the house and searched the street for Peter. He owed her lots of favors; he could get the ham for her. She spotted him with his pal, Willie Janzen, behind a tree stump, pretending to shoot at the soldier's backs.

"Peter!" Anna scolded. Willie jumped and his pale face turned a fiery red under his curly blond hair, but Peter didn't even glance up.

"Hi, Anna," Willie mumbled, nervously shaking out his "gun fingers" and trying to act as if he had just been innocently strolling past.

"Hello, Willie." Anna tried to smile through angrily clenched teeth. She wiped the stringy wisps of hair out of her eyes and shifted the bundle of sheets to her other arm, waiting for Peter to respond.

"Oh," Willie remembered suddenly. "My sister said to say hello if I saw you and . . ." he wrinkled his eyebrows trying to remember the rest of the message.

Anna shifted impatiently. "Tell Margaret I'll come to see her tomorrow."

"Oh, sure. Um . . . would you like help with those?" He pointed to the sheets.

"No, thank you, Willie. They're not heavy."

Willie nodded as Peter rolled his eyes.

Sometimes she didn't understand how the two could possibly be best friends. Shy, overly polite Willie, and Peter—increasingly mischievous and troublesome Peter. And Willie was a year younger too. Anna supposed it had something to do with the fact that they were the only two boys over twelve who still attended the village school. Anna knew that if Peter hadn't had Willie, school would have been unbearable for him. She still couldn't understand their friendship outside the school yard though.

Anna poked Peter in the shoulder and looked at him sternly. "What would Papa say to this game of yours?"

"Pa hunts with a gun," Peter said, shrugging carelessly.

"Not for people!"

"Well, Papa won't find out," Peter said threateningly, "because if he does, I'll tell him what you have hidden under your mattress. And how you got it."

Anna turned away and stormed back to the smokehouse. She never should have shared her secret with Peter. He just couldn't be trusted anymore. Now she would have to find a new hiding place for her pouch. And she would have to get the ham herself. She paused. Unless . . . Anna scanned the orchard trees for her sister. Susie didn't owe her any favors, but she could be tricked into doing anything. Anna would just have to make a game of it.

"Anna!" Mama's voice rang from the kitchen.

"Oh!" Anna stomped her foot. She couldn't see Susie anywhere, and she didn't have time to look for her. Anna set the sheets on a patch of grass and plugged her nose. She counted, the way she always did, how many seconds it took her to run in, snatch the meat, and run back out. As the door slammed on the smelly pigs, she stopped counting. "Nine seconds," she congratulated herself as she scooped up the sheets with her free hand.

When Anna finally ran into the house, Mama impatiently took the ham from her. Anna dropped the sheets onto the table and ran to the bedroom.

"What about your sister?" Mama called after her.

"I didn't see her. I'll go look again in just a moment," Anna called back. She snatched the small pouch from under her mattress and looked around the small room. The dresser drawers held Susie's aprons and stockings. If Susie found it, she would tell everyone she knew. Papa had just nailed down all the loose floorboards, and Mama cleaned the windowsill too often. Anna looked at Peter's unmade bed. Maybe that would be the safest place. Peter would never think to look under his own mattress. But then again, if he did, he might just claim that it was on his property and so it belonged to him. Under little Lizzy's crib was the only other place.

Oh, that would never do. Elizabeth would soon be toddling. No hiding place would be safe then.

"Anna!"

Anna stuffed the pouch into her apron. She would find a place later.

Chapter 2

Peter's Battle

"Why are you so jittery, Peter?" Mama asked, watching him spring from the window to the door and back again that evening. "You're too old to be bouncing around like that."

"Pa's late," he complained, dropping with a sigh and a thud on the kitchen chair. "When is he coming?"

"Soon," Mama said, then gave Peter stern warning looking. "But don't you bother him about the soldiers."

"But Ma!"

"Here he comes," Susie sang, smirking at Peter from her perch by the window.

Mama held up a warning finger. "Not a word," she said firmly as Papa pushed open the creaky door.

Before Papa even had a chance to breathe in the savory smell of fried ham, garden carrots, and fresh buns, his children surrounded him with excited hugs and kisses. His tired eyes brightened as each of the children filled his ears with stories of their day. Only Peter stood in the corner sullenly.

After giving Papa a bear hug, Anna went to Peter. "I'm sorry for getting angry," she whispered. "In front of Willie, I mean. I won't really tell Papa."

Peter nodded, impatient for the sentimental moment to end.

"You won't tell either?" she asked. Keeping secrets from Papa made her heart and her stomach hurt, but explaining what was in her pouch would be too difficult.

For a moment, Peter looked as though he had forgotten his threat. "I won't tell," he finally replied. "But I think you're wasting your time stealing that money."

"I'm not stealing!" she whispered sharply. "Mama and Papa will get it back. It's for their own good."

Peter rolled his eyes the way he often did lately.

"You'll never save enough," he insisted. "What do you want to go to Canada for anyway?"

Anna stared at him, wide-eyed and speechless. How could he even ask such a thing? It was what they all dreamed of. Even little Henry talked of cake in Canada. They were going to go there someday—even if Anna had to get them all there herself. And with her pouchful of money, she would. If only she could keep it secret until she had enough. Telling Papa would mean making it available for whatever needs he deemed necessary. And with Papa, that could be anything.

Before Anna could ask Peter what he was thinking, Papa came over. "What's the big secret?" He grinned at his two oldest children.

"Nothing very important," Peter lied. Anna bit her bottom lip and shrugged, not daring to look into Papa's eyes.

"Well, then, let's help Mama get supper."

"Yes, sir," they mumbled together. Anna shot Peter a warning glance as they hurried to get supper onto the table.

Susie chattered through the entire meal about her friends at school, about who didn't learn their Bible verses in Russian and who got the strap for cheating, and about how many kids had new hair ribbons and why didn't she? Papa finally cleared his throat and pushed back his chair, signaling that he wished to speak. Susie bit her tongue to keep it still.

"I heard some disturbing news today," he began as Mama poured him a cup of black barley coffee. "The Penner boy has disappeared. His papa came into the church today. He's deeply concerned."

"But he's gone off before, hasn't he?" Anna asked. "He always comes back." She knew about Jacob Penner. At seventeen years of age, he caused plenty of grief for his elderly parents.

Papa nodded. "Well, yes," he agreed hesitantly. "But this time he had a sack full of guns with him."

"Oh, dear God, no," Mama gasped, with her eyes raised to heaven and her hands clasped to her chest. Anna choked on her bun and Susie, for once, was speechless.

"Where did Jacob get them?" Peter asked. Anna heard an alarming note of interest in his voice and glared at him. Papa didn't seem to notice.

"It seems some passing soldiers left them. They told Jacob to get a group together and defend the village."

"They know that we don't fight," Mama said, angrily pushing her chair back from the table. She began gathering the dishes, clanging them together and muttering under her breath. Anna grabbed the rest of her bun before Mama could whisk it away too.

"They know," Papa agreed. "But they don't understand—or care."

"I don't understand either," Peter mumbled into his soup bowl. The kitchen was swallowed in sickly silence for a moment; then Peter boldly looked up at his astonished parents and spoke quickly. "Why don't we fight? Will we let the soldiers come and take away our money and our food? Maybe even our lives? Who will protect us if we don't protect ourselves?"

"God has always protected us, son," Papa answered calmly. "He brought us to Russia and gave us this land."

"He didn't protect Aaron, did he?" Peter himself cringed after he said it and looked down again into his soup. Nobody dared look at Mama.

"Peter," Papa asked. "Who is it you want to fight—the Russian army or God?"

Peter sat again in silence. He didn't seem to have an answer.

Papa stood and looked directly into his son's angry eyes. "If you should see young Jacob or hear about his hiding place, you will tell me directly. And you will have nothing to do with him, do you understand?" Papa spoke clearly and forcefully.

Peter eyes flashed. He stood at his spot and leaned on the table. There was a frightening excitement in his voice. "If you would just let me quit school, Papa. Then I could defend Mama and the little ones while you're away all day. Then at least I would feel like I'm doing something! At school, I'm no good to anyone."

"You will get an education," Papa said; then he went outside without finishing his meal. Mama followed.

"What is wrong with you?" Anna scolded, gathering up the rest of the dirty dishes. She had no appetite left for her bun now. "Papa is the pastor in this village. How can you even think about pretending to fight this war? You are only fifteen years old and it is not our war. We are not Russian!"

"Speak for yourself," Peter mumbled, falling back into his chair in defeat. "I like Russia."

"Russia is what killed your brother, Peter! Do you think Aaron would want you to fight in this war?"

"It wasn't Russia that killed him, Anna. It was those blasted Maschka flies in the logging camp. It's not Russia's fault that he's allergic to them. It's God's."

Anna felt her heart leap into her throat. "It's Russia's fault that he was in that logging camp in the first place. When our people settled here, Russia promised that we would never have to take part in their wars. They promised, and then they broke that promise when they made Aaron and the others work in the logging camps and the hospitals. It wasn't our fight then, and it's not our fight now. You spend too much time with those Russian boys from the factory school. You think like them now."

"Good. The Russian kids know more about this war than any

of our people do. They know about a lot of things. Papa wants me to go to the little village school, keep my nose in his precious German books, and learn how to be a good Mennonite, but there's a lot more to life than that. This world is big. This country is big. If learning is so important to Papa, he should be glad that I'm learning as much as I can about everything."

Anna angrily tried to shake the tears from her eyes as she began to wash dishes. Peter came to her side after a moment. His voice had softened a little. "Anna," he said, "surely even you have heard about Nestor Makhno and his band, and what they're doing. They've nearly destroyed villages just like ours—"

"I don't want to hear about it."

But Peter kept talking. "Fire and typhoid fever," he continued. "Murder and looting. . . . They don't care who are Russians or Germans. They don't care if we worship God or the czar—"

"The czar is dead," Anna reminded him and sniffed.

"That's just what I mean. They already killed him. Why shouldn't they kill us too? Don't you think somebody should do something?"

"I don't think it should be you," she answered harshly, nearly scrubbing the glaze right off the plates. She closed her eyes to shut out the horrible stories she had heard about the terror named Makhno, but her mind suddenly filled with visions of burning homes and people being slain in their beds. She had forced herself to believe that the terror he had shed around the villages existed only in stories made up to entice the Mennonites to fight. In Peter's case, it had worked, and it would take a miracle to calm the hatred in his heart. Silently, he went to his room and shut himself in.

Later that night, when Peter went out to chop wood, Anna sat down beside Papa and the comforting fire. "Papa," she said quietly. "Tell me more about Nestor Makhno and his band, the Makhnovstky."

Papa looked at her and frowned. "Makhno and his band is no concern of yours, liebling," he said. "He is a man full of hatred, but his anger is toward the powerful and the rich, not us. He terrorizes those with money to spare and those with many servants. Especially those who mistreat their servants." Then Papa laughed out loud. "That is no worry for us. We are as safe as the crows in our old forest." Anna had to smile. Papa had never complained about their lack of money, but for once in his life, he actually seemed glad to be poor.

Anna thought of her pouch, now safely hidden. "Soon we will be safer even than that," she wanted to tell Papa, but the time didn't seem right yet.

"Let me tell you instead," Papa continued, "about the God who will keep us safe through this dreadful war. . . ." Papa opened his old, treasured Bible and filled her ears with warm stories of God's hand over his people. Occasionally, he glanced outside, to where Peter sat on a stack of logs, whittling sticks, and his eyes glazed over with sadness.

If only Peter would sit and listen, for once.

Chapter 3

Gypsy Trail

The other girls crowded around Anna in the playground as she held out the shiny coin for them to see. Anna set aside her tin lunch pail, too excited to eat the ham sandwich and apple pie that her mother had packed. She had never won anything before in her life, and now she glowed.

"I wish I was as good as you in arithmetic," her best friend, Margaret, sighed. "If I had won that contest I would use all the money to buy sugar, and I would lick the bag clean, and I wouldn't share a bit of it." The other girls nodded and sighed dreamily as they continued to stare at Anna's coin.

The arithmetic contest had been difficult for most of them—that's why their teacher had promised them a prize—but it had been simple for Anna; she could multiply faster than anyone. Her father said it came from counting the coins in the freedom jar a hundred times a day. As Anna remembered the empty clay jar, she felt a sharp stab of anger.

"Well, one day," she silently promised herself, "when I'm in charge of all the money in the candy factory, I'm not giving it to anybody."

"What will you buy with it?" the girls asked, still staring at her shiny new coin.

Anna smiled sheepishly as she thought about her leather pouch in its new hiding place. Nobody but Margaret knew about her plans.

"It's a secret," she said and was drowned in pleas and whines from the others. "Oh, don't be angry," she begged. "I'll tell you someday. I promise."

"I know what she's going to do with it!" a voice called from behind.

Anna spun to see Hildi Voth standing a few feet away with her pale, delicate arms crossed smugly and her perfectly pointed chin in the air. Her auburn braids hung tight and straight, tied with finely starched ribbon to match her costly green dress. But today, even Hildi's shiny new boots and delicate silk stockings didn't embarrass Anna, who's ribbon never lasted until lunch and whose boots had more mud than shine to them. Anna was one coin closer to Canada today. Nothing else mattered.

"Mind your own business," Margaret sneered at Hildi.

"That coin will buy food for your family for three weeks, won't it, Crow?" Hildi taunted. The name didn't hurt Anna the way Hildi always hoped it would. Anna was proud to be named for the night-black birds that played in the forest where she and Peter had been born. She still remembered the way they flew around their heads and danced at her feet, then disappeared above the trees when they grew tired of playing. Sometimes Anna wished she really were a crow. Then she could fly away to Canada without any money at all. She could just go—whenever she wanted.

"Go jump in the creek, Hildi," Margaret jeered. "You're just jealous that you didn't win."

"I don't have to know arithmetic," Hildi laughed. "I'm not going to be a shopkeeper." She said the word shopkeeper as though it were a dirty word and then smirked at Margaret, whose father worked in the general store.

"That's a good thing," Anna finally spoke up, unable to stay silent another second. "Because then you would have to know how to add two plus two."

Hildi stuck out her ugly tongue and turned toward the swings where her only friend, Sarah, waited.

"How can she tease you like that when everyone knows she has a crush on your brother? I bet she wouldn't call him Crow," one of the girls said in disgust.

"She probably thinks Peter is secretly a prince that your family found in the woods," Margaret laughed.

"He looks like a prince," said a shy girl with twinkles in her eyes.

"Rose!" Margaret shrieked. Rose blushed and the other girls giggled. Anna shifted uncomfortably. She didn't want to talk about her brother. If these girls only knew how unlike a prince he really was, they would shudder.

"Well, even if Peter is a prince, Hildi is nothing even close to a princess. So don't let her bother you," Margaret said.

"She doesn't bother me today," Anna said truthfully. "She's not going to ruin my day." The only thing Anna regretted about this day was that she wouldn't be able to tell her parents that she had won. If she told them, they would want to know her plans for the money and she couldn't tell them that yet. It had to be a perfect surprise for the day she handed them all the money for the trip. She got shivers thinking about it.

That reminds me of something, she thought, then whispered to Margaret, "I'll be right back."

Around the back of the schoolhouse, Peter and Willie were tossing iron horseshoes at sticks poking out of the ground. In her hurry, Anna didn't notice Peter aiming for a toss, and she called his name just as he let his ring go. It clanged against a rock two feet from the pole and rolled down a hill toward the school walls.

"Anna!"

"Sorry." Anna cringed, and Willie snickered.

Peter glared at Willie, who stopped smiling instantly, then turned angrily toward his sister. "What do you want?"

"Could I talk to you a minute?"

"What?"

Anna looked at Willie, who waited patiently for the game to begin again.

"Alone, please," she added quietly.

Peter rolled his eyes. "Back in a minute," he muttered, tossing the rest of his rings at Willie's feet and kicking at the stick as he passed it. Willie nodded agreeably as the two wandered off toward the woodshed at the back of the school.

"Aren't you going to congratulate me?"

"For what?"

Anna held out her hand to reveal the coin.

"Oh, yeah, I guess you did all right." he nodded. "Maybe you should do my homework from now on." Then he looked at her suspiciously. "But that better not be the reason you messed up my throw."

Anna shook her head. "I just wanted to tell you not to . . ." Anna hesitated. She didn't want any of his questions today. "Just don't tell Mama and Papa about this, all right?" Peter looked at her strangely. "I want to save it," she confided. "I want it to be a surprise."

"Sure," he shrugged. Anna could tell he still thought she was crazy. "Can I go back to my game now?"

❧

Anna sat in her place on the long wooden class bench for the rest of the afternoon, but her mind was far away in Canada, with Johnny and her dreams. The chalkboard became just a blur of chalky squiggles as her head filled with imagined moments of joy—the moment she gave her parents all the money and the moment she saw Johnny again. When the teacher asked her to recite a Bible verse, Anna couldn't even remember the first word, and the teacher threatened to take back the prize coin. Anna could think of nothing but the new coin and her trip to freedom. She still didn't have nearly as much as the jar used to hold, but she had a beginning—more than she would have had if she hadn't done anything. When the teacher finally dismissed them for the day, Anna raced down the rickety, wooden steps into the sunshine.

"Hey, wait!" Margaret called to her.

Anna stopped and turned back toward the school. Margaret skipped down the stairs and ran across the playground to Anna. "Where are you going?" she puffed, wide-eyed, and pointed down the road that Anna headed toward. "You can't go that way!"

Anna hesitated. She always walked the other way with Margaret, toward Margaret's home, and then turned off on the windy road to her house. It was safer, they were sure. The other path home went by the old overgrown apple grove and the creek. Beyond those trees stood a gypsy camp. Many of the kids had seen the strange gypsies watching with curious eyes, and parents had warned the children not to bother them. They never said why, but everybody knew: Gypsies ate little children. Occasionally, Anna and Margaret would measure themselves on Margaret's door and wonder if they were big enough to pass the gypsy camp safely. Each time, they decided not quite—but soon. It was much safer to go the way of Margaret's house, but it took longer, and today Anna didn't want to waste time.

"I'm going to go the short way," she informed Margaret, whose eyes grew bigger and rounder.

"Do you think it's safe?" she whispered.

Anna nodded bravely. "I'll go very fast."

"Do you want me to go with you?" Margaret swallowed a lump of fear in her throat. When Anna said no, Margaret sighed with relief and hugged Anna good-bye, as though she might never see her again. Anna couldn't help but laugh.

"You worry too much, Margaret," she said. "I'll be fine, really."

The girls waved and went off in opposite directions. Not many people traveled the road Anna had taken. *Maybe even the adults are afraid of the gypsies*, she thought as her heart began racing.

"Oh, don't be silly," she told herself. She said it out loud, just so she wouldn't feel so alone. "There is no reason for grown-ups to come this way." In her head, she started listing all the reasons for them not to: the shops and factories were the other direction; this road was rockier and narrower; it was a longer route for most of them. As she passed the path that branched into the grove—Gypsy Trail—she held her breath. She wanted to sing, to make the road feel cheerier, but she didn't want to draw attention to herself. When something rustled in the bush, Anna darted as fast as she could. She thought she heard footsteps behind her too, but she didn't dare stop and look again. Almost out of breath, Anna passed the church and soon reached her house safely.

Before going in, she ran to the tree at the side of their house. Mama's laundry line was tied to it and wet clothes flapped in the breeze, but Mama was nowhere in sight. High up in the tree was a small, empty bird's nest from two springs ago. Anna stretched to feel inside and carefully pulled out the leather pouch. It was the best hiding place she had found yet. She pulled from her dress pocket the shiny new coin and placed it deep in the pouch before stuffing it back into the nest, confident that her hiding place was still a secret. Anna was so busy dreaming about Canada that she didn't notice movement behind the barn across the street.

Chapter 4

Borrowed Coins

There had been no more bomb scares from attack planes, and the soldiers left the village a few days later. Some villagers were relieved to see them go. Others worried that the Red Army might take their place.

"At least the White Army behaved decently when staying in the villagers' homes," Mama sighed. "Even if they did eat too much."

Anna had other things on her mind though. "Mama?" she asked early on Saturday morning. "May Susie and I go to the market for you today? And the post office?" Anna would have liked to go alone, but she needed the extra hand to carry the market goods.

Susie looked up from her sewing. "I need to finish these stockings before tomorrow," she whined. Anna looked at Susie's first pair of stockings. Susie was proud of her work, but Anna groaned to herself. If Susie showed up at school wearing those, Hildi would surely have something awful to say about her family again.

"We can go quickly," Anna assured Susie, "and then I'll help you with your stockings." That would solve both problems.

"All right," Susie sighed and put her project down.

"Why are you in such a rush to go?" Mama asked suspiciously, but Anna had an answer already prepared.

"I'm sure there must be a letter from Johnny today," she said. "And I don't want to wait until you are ready."

"Are you sure the two of you can carry it all?"

Before Susie could complain, Anna promised they could manage it fine. Mama gave the girls the market money and a list, and sent them on their way.

Anna moved slowly, waiting for just the right moment, and as soon as they were far enough away from the house, she stopped. "Oh, I forgot to ask if Mama needed sugar!" she said.

"It's right here on the list," Susie pointed out.

"Does it say how much?"

"No, but doesn't she always get—"

"Just go ask," Anna interrupted impatiently. "You're a faster runner, you go back and I'll keep walking. You can catch up."

Susie faltered. She was proud of her ability to run fast, although Mama constantly reminded her of how unladylike it was. She clearly couldn't see the point of running back this time though. Anna watched her struggle with the decision. "Just hurry up and go," Anna prodded until Susie finally huffed in exasperation and sprinted back toward the house. Anna quickly looked through the small purse of money Mama had given them. How much could she take without Mama noticing?

Anna heard Susie's steps racing back and took out one of the smallest coins and stuffed it into her apron pocket.

"The same as always," Susie reported, puffing too hard to say anything more for at least a few minutes. Anna smugly and silently congratulated herself on that. Having Susie silent was a bonus she hadn't thought of when she made her run back. And she needed that silence. It gave her time to convince herself that she wasn't really stealing. By the time they reached the village square market, Anna was satisfied. She was saving the money to surprise her family. That was the furthest thing from stealing.

"Hey!" Susie pointed toward the blacksmith shop. "There's Peter."

Peter and Willie were heading out of the shop with a sack.

"Thank you, Mr. Dyck!" they called as they ran off out of town.

"I thought he was supposed to be cleaning out the pig barn," Anna said.

"He did it already," Susie informed her. "Before milking the cows."

"Really?" Anna looked at her in surprise. Peter hated mornings more than anything, and he usually put off his Saturday chores until as late as possible. In fact, he often didn't even get the cows milked before the herder came to take them to pasture. That always meant he had to take them himself, and he hated that. What could be so important that he would get the cows milked and the barn cleaned before she even woke up?

"Come on," Anna said, a part of her feeling pleased to see him happy. It had been days since he had smiled. She tried to convince herself that it meant things were all right again. A nagging feeling, however, told her that maybe it wasn't. "Let's get the market done," she mumbled.

With a little luck, Anna was able to get everything on Mama's list without the missing money. The post office had nothing for her though. She didn't really expect them to. It had been an awfully long time since a letter had come. Anna tried to push Johnny from her mind. She didn't need one more thing to worry about right now. Maybe, she assured herself, the letter would come next week.

"You take these in," Anna instructed Susie when they returned home. She handed over her basket of groceries. "I want to do something."

Susie grumbled but obeyed, and Anna raced to the tree to hide her coin. She reached in and felt around. Twice she stretched her fingers into the nest, but they came out empty.

The pouch was gone!

Chapter 5

Margaret's House

"Mama!" Anna hollered, running into the house.

"Hush!" Mama quieted her. "The babies are sleeping."

"Mama, were you up in the tree this morning?" As soon as she said it, she knew how ridiculous it sounded.

Mama looked at her strangely. "I certainly was not," she replied. "Why?"

"No reason, I guess," Anna sighed. "I lost something up there."

"Well, maybe your friend knows about it," Mama said. "She was in the yard today while you were at the market. Did you forget you were supposed to meet her there?"

Anna couldn't remember planning any meetings with Margaret. "Can I run over and see her?" Anna asked.

"Maybe later," Mama said. "You have another job to do right now." She pointed to Susie working hard on her stockings again.

Anna groaned to herself.

"And when that's done, I'd like you to bathe the little ones for church tomorrow."

"Yes, ma'am." Anna sighed and dropped on the sofa beside Susie.

"Here, just let me do it," she said, impatiently snatching the stockings from Susie. She looked them over carefully and shook her head. The large, crooked stitches made the stockings look like they belonged in the orphan bag. Or like they had just come out of it.

"Why don't you just wear my stockings tomorrow," Anna suggested.

"And what will you wear?" Mama asked from the corner where she sat darning socks.

"It's warm enough. I'll go without stockings. Who will notice?"

Mama gave her a look that didn't need an answer, so Anna impatiently began the tedious task of finishing the stitches and trying to fix the ones that were already done.

She finished the stockings and the baths with just enough time to run to Margaret's before dinner. When she stumbled into the small front yard, where Margaret stood hanging laundry, she was out of breath.

"Hi there!" Margaret waved dramatically to Anna with a white handkerchief. "Why are you puffing?"

Anna flopped on the tree stump next to the clothesline. "I ran all the way"—Anna panted, and took two deep breaths—"to see why you were at my house this morning."

"Not me," Margaret said, pointing to the full basket of clean, wet clothes. "I've been doing these all day long. See, just look at my hands. They look like prunes. Thomas Junior gets so dirty, I think it would be easier to sew him new pants than to clean these, but—"

Anna held up a hand to stop Margaret's rambling. She took one more hearty breath. "You weren't in my yard?"

Margaret shook her head just as her mother stepped outside. "Anna!" she said clapping her hands together. "It's so good to see you. Now don't run off before I can get some of our apples to send back with you. I so enjoyed your father's sermon on Sunday about sharing that I've turned over a new leaf and I'm going to start by giving your mother some of my apples, unless of course you have enough, in which case . . ."

Anna fidgeted impatiently as Mrs. Janzen talked and talked and talked. She could hardly believe that Willie—bashful, silent Willie—came from the same family as these two chatterboxes. When Mrs. Janzen had at last finished talking, Anna couldn't even remember what she had started out talking about.

When Mrs. Janzen stared at her questioningly, Anna stuttered, "Um, uh, pardon?"

"I said, could your mama use some apples?" she asked again, more slowly.

"Oh, yes, ma'am, thank you. I think so anyway. The birds ate most of ours again." Inwardly, Anna groaned. That would mean another full day in the hot kitchen making applesauce and apple kuchen, but at least Mrs. Janzen would leave them alone for a moment, while she fetched them.

"Fine then, I'll go get a basket." Mrs. Janzen disappeared into the whitewashed house, and Anna slumped back on the tree stump.

"What am I going to do?" she wailed. Then she quickly told Margaret the whole story.

"Oh, Anna! Your new coin!" Margaret almost began to cry.

"And other coins too." Anna confessed. "I found one under a market stall last week and I earned a couple from the barbershop that week when I filled in for Peter, sweeping up. And there were some that I, uh, borrowed from Mama." Anna had never told Margaret about those ones.

"We'll find them," Margaret assured her. "We'll get a detective or a spy and—"

"Here are those apples," Mrs. Janzen called out, joining the girls in the yard. "You'd better hurry home with them, Anna. It must be almost time for your supper. Now Margaret . . ." Mrs. Janzen began scolding Margaret then, about some stains on the laundry, so Anna couldn't speak another word about her pouch.

"Thank you," Anna called over the loud voice of Margaret's mother. Mrs. Janzen waved without even taking a breath. Anna glanced back anxiously at Margaret, who promised again, with a smile and a nod, that they would figure something out. Then she turned back to her mother, and Anna had no choice but to leave without a plan. The walk home dragged painfully slow. Her basket was heavy and her mind was heavier. Where could her money be?

Supper had begun as Anna came into the kitchen. She was glad to have the heavy apples to blame for being late. She dropped them on the counter with a quick explanation, then sat at her place to eat.

"Mama," she asked the moment there was a lull in Susie's incessant chatter, "who did you say came by this afternoon?"

"She said she was a friend of yours. I didn't recognize her. From one of the big houses, I imagine, by the way she was dressed. I don't think I've ever seen her at church. Pretty girl, but a little forward. Beautiful hair ribbons though."

Anna nearly dropped her fork.

Hildi.

Chapter 6

A Risky Deal

 "**P**eter!" Anna raced away the minute dinner ended. Peter had already excused himself and gone to the barn.

"Peter?" she peeked in the barn door, expecting to see him shining his shoes for church. A noise up in the loft startled her.

"Peter?" Anna said again, as she climbed the ladder and poked her head up to see. Peter sat hunched over, engrossed in a pile of loose metal and wood bits. His unshined shoes lay in the straw beside him. He didn't hear her coming and didn't see her watching him.

"What are you doing?" she finally asked.

Peter jumped with a start and fumbled with the tools in his hand, trying to hide the odd bunch of stuff in front of him.

"I'm building something," he stammered as he crammed it all into the sack beside him. "What do you want?"

"My money," she said, still eyeing the sack. "It's gone."

"Well, I didn't take it," he answered, clearly anxious for her to go.

"I know. I think Hildi took it."

"Hildi? Why would she want your little coins? She probably has a hundred of her own."

"Because she's jealous." Anna had figured it all out already. She didn't need the money, Peter was right about that, but she didn't like to lose, and she certainly didn't like to be laughed at. "I did a dumb thing," Anna continued. "I said something mean about her after she teased me about the money. Everybody laughed at her."

"That was dumb," Peter agreed. "Hildi doesn't like to be laughed at."

"But how can I get it back?" Anna wailed. Then she remembered something important.

"Hildi likes you, you know," she told Peter.

"Of course, I know," Peter answered with disgust. "She's an awful pest."

"But do you suppose that, maybe you can pretend to like her back, just to get my money?"

"Not in a million years!" Peter insisted. "She'll put a collar and a leash on me in no time. I'm not gonna be no pet of hers."

Anna rolled her eyes impatiently. There had to be a way. She inched closer to the sack, and Peter grabbed it out of her reach. "What are you building?" she asked.

"A tool."

"A tool?" Anna looked doubtful. It didn't look like any tool she had ever seen. "Well, if you get my money back, I'll give you some of it. You could buy more parts for your tool." Anna knew right away that she had a hit a sensitive spot. He needed money. She could see it in his eyes.

"How much?" he asked.

"A kopchen." The one she had taken from Mama should be enough. She could get another one next week.

"I'll try," he finally mumbled. "But if she tries to lead me around by her aprons strings, the whole deals off! And I want something for trying."

"Oh, thank you, thank you!" Anna kissed him excitedly and ran back to the house. Peter would think of something brilliant. That was the brother she loved.

Anna watched Peter in church the next day as he sang in the

choir. Even though he hated singing, he had a beautiful voice. And it grew deeper, it seemed, every week. She supposed it wasn't that strange for Hildi to have a crush on him. Johnny used to stand right next to Peter in the choir. He was even more handsome. Hildi always had a crush on Johnny too, ever since she was eight and found out about the candy he had shared with Anna. But Johnny didn't like her one bit. He would never share his candy with Hildi. The only girl he ever talked to was Anna. That had always made Hildi hate Anna more.

If Johnny hadn't left, he could tell her what to do about her money. One thing was for sure: Anna would never ask Johnny to be nice to Hildi.

For four days after that, Anna watched Hildi carefully at school. She didn't dare talk to her though. She knew she would say something horrible and ruin everything.

"Doesn't it bother you to see them together?" Margaret asked on the fourth day, nodding toward Peter and Hildi, who were eating their lunch together. Anna had to admit that he had been putting in a real effort. Some of their classmates had even noticed and started to make jokes about it. "What if he decides he likes her better than you—his own sister—and he lets her keep the money? It could happen, you know."

"Don't be ridiculous," Anna snapped at her. "That would never happen." But in her heart, Anna wasn't so sure. Hildi could be charming when she wanted to. And with Peter she clearly wanted to. She may have a pretty face, Anna seethed to herself, but everything else about her is ugly as pig slop. Putting Peter up to this had been a big mistake. Hildi didn't deserve Peter's friendship, even if it was only pretend friendship. And Peter didn't deserve her either, regardless of how awful he had been recently.

On the fifth day, when Peter and Hildi sat huddled in a secret talk by the swings, Anna couldn't stand it anymore. "Peter!"

she called and started to march over to him. *It's not worth it*, she thought. *I'll find a different way.* They both saw her coming, and Hildi slipped her hand into Peter's for just a second and ducked off behind the school.

Peter sauntered toward Anna and handed her the leather pouch.

"It's all there," he assured her.

"Thanks, Peter! How did you do it?" she asked. Knowing that Peter was free of Hildi felt almost as great as holding the coins again and hearing them clink in the pouch.

Peter blushed a little and shrugged. "It was nothing," he said. "Just don't lose it again."

"I didn't lose it," she reminded him, but he just shrugged and turned away.

"Wait," Anna opened the pouch to get the promised coin for Peter.

"You don't have to pay me," he said with a smile before rushing off again.

After lunch, in the classroom, Anna looked down the row of seats for Hildi, but she wasn't around. Peter's spot on the boys' side was empty too.

"Anna," the teacher said as the children settled into their seats on both sides of the long table, "where has your brother gone to?"

Anna wished she knew the answer to that. She looked to his friends in the back for help. They shrugged and snickered.

"He must have gone home," she stuttered nervously and then added, "he looked a little flushed."

The teacher nodded and turned to the blackboard. From the back, Anna heard one of the boys mutter, "Yeah, so did Hildi." Then they snickered some more.

Chapter 7

Backfire!

Peter never returned to school that day. Neither did Hildi. By the end of the day, the pouch in Anna's pocket seemed heavier than a stack of bricks.

Because of these few coins, she thought, *Peter has got himself into some kind of trouble with that horrid Hildi!*

"Where do you think Peter and Hildi went?" Margaret asked, as they walked home after school. Anna had gone back to walking the longer road with Margaret.

"Oh, Margaret!" Anna wailed, unable to keep it in any longer. "It's all my fault!" She remembered what Peter had said about a leash and collar. "She probably has him tied up in her basement."

Margaret stifled a laugh. "Perhaps she's eaten him already," she teased and then, seeing the shock on Anna's face added, "Oh, Anna! He's fine. She probably invited him to her house for 'sweets and tea.'" Margaret tossed her long braids over her shoulder and batted her eyelashes. "That's what the fancy ladies do with their captives, you know," she mocked.

Anna couldn't help but smile at Margaret's flamboyant imitation. Her mouth watered at the thought of sweets. "I guess it's too much to hope that he'll bring some sweets home for me, isn't it?"

"You're impossible." Margaret shook her head as she turned onto her yard then looked back at Anna with another toss of her hair. "Would you like to join me for tea and . . . and well . . . apples, I guess," she added with a disappointed twist of her nose.

"No, thank you," Anna laughed. "I'd like to get home and see what Peter's got up to."

"Farewell then." Margaret waved grandly as Anna continued down the dirt road toward home. The busy afternoon traffic had begun and the noise in the street was so loud and distracting that she didn't hear her name being called. She gasped when someone grabbed her arm firmly from behind.

"Willie!" she cried when she saw who it was. It was so out of character for him that it frightened her a little. "You're hurting me!" she said, wrenching her arm away.

"Sorry, Anna," he puffed as he tried to catch his breath. He was panting as though he had run a great distance.

"What's the matter?"

Willie could barely catch his breath, much less speak, but he was able to squeak out one word: "Peter." He motioned for her to follow, and Anna raced back with him toward the schoolhouse.

Behind the school, Willie led her to a large wooded area that backed onto a farmer's field. A pyramid of tin cans teetered on the fence post, and propped up against a large tree lay Peter spattered with blood. Kneeling next to him, as white as a ghost, was Hildi, doing her best to stop the bleeding with her perfectly starched hair ribbons.

Peter looked weakly at her, but didn't speak.

"The worst of it has stopped," Hildi informed Willie. She wouldn't look at Anna. "But he's lost a lot of blood."

Anna whipped off her apron and tore it to shreds, tossing them one by one to Hildi, who wound them around the flowing wounds.

"What happened?" Anna finally choked out. Her tone was sharp and accusing. Nobody answered, but they all looked at each other with panicked eyes. It must be worse than she thought. Then she saw the answer to her question on the ground a few feet away. There lay Peter's mysterious tool. But now it looked strangely like a gun. An unusual gun with many of the pieces scattered around, but definitely a gun.

I guess he didn't need my money, after all, she thought to herself. And then it all made sense. Hildi. In that moment, before she had time to question either of them, Peter passed out.

"We have to get him home," Anna instructed, even though her heart pounded ferociously in her throat. After checking that Peter's heart was still pounding too, she stood. This would mean trouble. Big trouble. If Peter survived.

"Do you think we can carry him?" Anna asked Willie.

"Sure," Willie answered as he crouched to grab Peter's shoulders. Then he stood and tossed a sack from under Peter's head, at Hildi. "Take the gun home with you," he instructed.

"What for?" Anna asked angrily, facing both of them with iron eyes. "You don't think you're going to try and repair that blasted thing, do you?"

Willie lay a gentle, calming hand on her shoulder as Hildi stuffed the weapon into the sack. "We can't leave it here, Anna," he told her in a strange voice. Then he turned to Hildi. "Bury it."

Hildi hesitated, clearly wanting to go with Peter, but Anna glared at her until she turned and ran the other way, clutching the sack.

Between them, Anna and Willie got Peter to the edge of the bush behind the schoolhouse. Nobody was in sight.

"We gotta go the quick way," Willie said. "Less people and faster too. You ain't scared are you?"

"No." It wasn't the gypsies that scared her this time. It was everybody else. What would they say when they found out?

They secured their grip on Peter and began the walk toward

Gypsy Trail. A strange noise came through the trees as they neared it and Willie slowed down a little.

"Oh, great," he muttered under his breath. "They're out."

Before she had time to think, a bedraggled bunch of men stepped off Gypsy Trail into the road ahead of them, only a hundred yards away. They seemed preoccupied with their conversation until they spotted the kids, standing lifeless on the path. Then they began to walk toward them. Anna thought, for a moment, that they looked concerned. Maybe they would help. But Willie didn't give her a chance to find out.

"Turn around, turn around," he prompted, swinging Peter's shoulders in the opposite direction. Anna turned with Peter's feet and shuffled back down the gravel road toward the school and the safer, longer, and busier road.

"People are going to ask questions," Anna said, slightly annoyed that she didn't even know the answer to those questions herself. She adjusted her hold and tried to keep up with Willy's long stride.

"Leave it to me," Willie insisted as they carried Peter onto the busier main street. They had hardly walked three feet when Willie and Margaret's father, on his way home, approached them, followed by two or three other men from the village. They circled the kids, pushing their way to Peter.

"What happened to the boy?" Mr. Janzen demanded, as he effortlessly took Peter's limp feet from Anna and started toward his house.

"He was up a tree," Willie started nervously, but nobody was listening. Both Willie and Anna had to almost sprint to keep up.

"Get the doctor," Mr. Janzen directed the other men. By this time a crowd had gathered. "We'll take him to my place. John. See if you can find his pa."

"I think I saw the reverend out in the churchyard," called another, who ran off in that direction.

Willie's eyes looked glazed over and sickly. His face was still pale too. He would have to answer their questions if Peter didn't wake up soon. What would he tell the doctor?

That opportunity came quickly. As soon as they had Peter lying on a bed in Willie and Margaret's house, the doctor came rushing in. Without his white coat and glasses, Anna hardly recognized him. His normally friendly, soothing face was wrinkled with concern, and his black bag hung open, packed hurriedly, with cloth bandages spilling over the sides.

"Who can tell me what's going on?" he asked quickly and firmly. Willie, who had been directed to the kitchen table, stood up and Anna tried to also, but Willie lay a firm hand on her shoulder and pushed her back down. "I'll do it," he promised, and he followed the doctor into the back room. Papa came a few moments later and went straight past Anna without a glance.

"The doctor will fix him," Margaret whispered assuredly, putting an arm around her shoulders.

Anna nodded absentmindedly, but her greatest fear wasn't for Peter's health. In her heart, she suspected that he'd recover. She had quickly felt for his heartbeat through his bloodied shirt once more before leaving him with the men. It hadn't been strong, but it was steady. Her concern was with a much bigger issue. And not even the wise doctor could help them with it.

Once the commotion died down and only Anna and Margaret's families remained in the kitchen, Papa poked his head out of the bedroom door and said solemnly, "He'll live. Go home, Anna." Anna felt judgment had been laid on her head as well. She cringed but didn't have a chance to defend herself before Papa disappeared back into the room.

Margaret took Anna by the hand. "Come on, I'll go with you," she whispered, then led Anna outside. The sun still blazed, though it seemed like days had passed in that silent kitchen. Anna had hoped to be gone from Russia by summer. Maybe if they had been gone, Peter would be fine.

"It was a gun, Margaret," she finally spoke in disbelief. "After all of Papa's warnings, he built himself a gun."

"How?"

"Bits and pieces. He must have found some parts and built the rest."

"And he shot himself?"

"I don't know exactly what happened," Anna confessed, "but I do know Hildi helped."

"Hildi shot him?"

"No! Well, at least, I don't think so. Peter needed money and I promised to give him some. And then, after he talked with Hildi, he didn't need my money anymore. The money was going to be for that gun."

"You were going to help him buy pieces for a gun?" Margaret still didn't understand.

"I didn't know. I thought it was a tool of some sort. That's what he told me."

"Wow. Peter's never lied to you before."

"I didn't think so, but now I don't know." Anna choked back a painful lump in her throat. "Maybe I never will."

Margaret placed a reassuring arm around Anna's waist. "Your papa said he'll live," she reminded her as they walked up to Anna's house.

"I know he'll live, Margaret," Anna choked. "I just don't know who he is anymore. I don't know if I can ever trust him again." Her mother, surrounded by other village women, came racing out of the house.

"Anna," she said breathlessly. "I'm going to Peter. Stay with the little ones; Susie's there now. And nobody is to go anywhere," she ordered, as though Anna were the one who had been in trouble. Then she dashed down the road and vanished.

Margaret stayed with Anna until sunset, when Mama and

Papa returned with Peter, who stubbornly and angrily walked on his own two feet. Anna dropped on the sofa in relief—and sorrow. His eyes were darker than ever before.

"Good-bye," Margaret mouthed to her as she waved quickly and slipping past the family and out of sight. As soon as she left, Peter was sent to his bed, and Papa quietly told Anna to sit at the table.

"Susie," Mama said, "take the babies outside to play."

Susie grumbled as she gathered the children slowly, hoping Papa would start to talk before she was out. Anna, on the other hand, hoped Papa wouldn't. She sensed that she was in some sort of trouble too.

Finally, Papa spoke. "Willie tells us that you knew nothing of this shameful accident. Is that the truth?"

"Yes, sir, that is . . . I mean, no sir," Anna stumbled over her words before spilling out the whole story of her part in stealing grocery money, and losing it, and bribing Peter to get it back. Finally, she broke into tears. "It's all my fault," she sniffed.

Mama put her hands on Anna's shoulders, and Papa hung his head.

"It's not all your fault," Papa told her. "But your deceit certainly played a part, didn't it?" Anna nodded and asked the question on her mind.

"What really happened?"

Papa sighed and stood up. "I guess you'll find out eventually," he said. "Everyone will." He stuffed his hands into his pockets and paced the room. "Peter built himself a gun, it seems," he said sadly. "Found some parts in the woods, got some from unknowing townsfolk, and built the rest. It seems he had some help from a young lady in your class."

So Willie had told on Hildi. Anna felt pleased that he had kept her own name out of it, even though she had helped too.

Papa continued. "When he tried to shoot—at a post or

something, I gather—the gun blew up." Papa swallowed hard and then said to himself, in an angry whisper, "Thanks be to the Lord that the girl wasn't closer!" Then he marched outside and slammed the door.

"May I see him?" Anna asked, and Mama nodded. "Briefly though."

When Anna peeked into the bedroom, Peter was reclined on the bed, staring blankly at the ceiling.

"I don't even want to know what you think," he said, without looking at her.

"Well, I want to know what you think," she retorted. "Or at least what you were thinking three hours ago."

"I already told you, and I'll tell you again," he said slowly. Even in his weakness, his eyes flashed. "Somebody's got to protect us. Jacob Penner and his group have the right idea, I tell you." He tried to sit, but fell back against the pillow. "Can you take a message to Hildi for me?"

Anna rolled her eyes.

"Just tell her I'm okay."

Anna didn't answer.

"She's not such a bad girl, Anna. I wish you two could just be friends. She said she likes you. Just doesn't think you like her. Couldn't you try? For me?"

"Never," Anna said with quiet force. "And I'm sorry I ever got you involved."

"I'm not," Peter said, then grimaced in pain. "Well, at least tell her I'm okay, would you? Please?"

"I don't know," Anna mumbled and left the room. Mama was beginning supper. Susie had brought the children in and was helping.

"Anna," Mama said, "set the table, please."

"Yes, ma'am," Anna answered. Hildi would have to wait. Maybe for a very long time.

Papa came in just as Anna set the last dish on the table. She had hoped that she would be sent out to get him, so that she could ask more questions, although she didn't exactly know what those questions would be. Seeing the strain in his eyes, however, she knew he wouldn't have any more answers for her today. Still she sat, hoping that he might have something encouraging to say once he had some of Mama's good cooking in his stomach. Papa surprised her though, by speaking up only seconds after he had said the grace.

"Children," he began quietly, "I have been offered a position as overseer at the seniors' home in another village. In light of our current situation, I have decided that we will take it. Next month, we shall move."

"But Papa!" Susie wailed. "I don't want to move! My friends are here."

"Hush," Mama warned her, but Papa raised a hand.

"It's all right," he told Mama. "They have a right to be angry. This whole family will be affected by the actions of one." Papa glanced at the closed bedroom door where Peter slept. "The Lord, I trust, has this whole dreadful event in his hands, but the fact remains: if a pastor cannot control the actions of his own son, he's not fit to manage an entire church."

"That's not true!" Anna protested, dropping her spoon into her soup. "You're a good pastor. Nobody will want to see you go. I'm sure of it. Just the other day, Margaret's mother told me what a good pastor you are."

Papa smiled. "Thank you for your confidence, Anna," he said patting her hand warmly. "But I think you will see that this is best. And the congregation will agree."

That settled it in Anna's mind. She wouldn't deliver Peter's message. She would never do anything for Peter again!

Chapter 8

Makhno Fire

The next week at school was the hardest week Peter and Anna had ever faced. Their friends mourned their upcoming move with showers of hugs and tears, while others openly condemned them for Peter's newly discovered thirst for violence. It hadn't taken long for the entire village to hear about the gun. Peter seemed to have no friends left, except for Willie and Hildi. The worst part was accepting that Papa had been right. Anna suspected that many parents had told their children to shun Peter—and her at the same time.

Yet for some reason, despite it all, Papa still insisted that Peter finish the last few weeks of school. Many arguments about Peter's schooling had followed that fateful night with the gun. Peter insisted that being in school had done him little good. Anna secretly agreed. It certainly hadn't kept him out of trouble, which she suspected was part of Papa's plan for having him in school. But Papa stood firm, insisting it was for Peter's own good. Anna didn't bother telling Papa that Peter didn't always show up. Hildi didn't always either. Anna scowled every time she thought of it, but held her tongue, hoping that the move would put distance between them. And when they did, their attention was on each other, not on reading and arithmetic.

At the end of the longest week of her life, Anna sat in the hard church pews and listened to her father's last sermon. He prayed, as always, for the safe passage of the many who were emigrating. It seemed everyone was losing someone these days to the ships heading for America. Anna thought of Johnny and closed her eyes tightly, trying to imagine him across the aisle in one of their pews. It had been two years since he had been a part of their life and their school and their church. How many more years, she wondered, before she would be a part of his.

The villagers didn't stand around after the Sunday service to shake Papa's hand and invite him for the traditional fastpa meal and tell him how wonderful he was. Most of them attended service, but the greetings afterward were brief and cold.

"Pastor." Some of them nodded, with a stiff lip.

"Good day," said others, without even looking into his eyes.

Many just squeezed past, pretending to be in a hurry to get home. Anna ran home by herself, unable to watch the change in the people she thought were their friends. How dare they blame Papa for Peter's waywardness! Papa always did his best! As for Peter, Anna would barely utter a word to him, and he didn't seem to notice. He disappeared daily into his own world, never even apologizing for the trouble he had caused.

Anna was already preparing the buns and cheese and sweets, when the others came into the kitchen. "Oh, this heat!" Mama exclaimed as she mopped her forehead with the apron on her dress. "How long has it been now since we've had rain?" she asked.

Papa looked out the window. "Months," he answered. "I think it's time to begin taking care. After lunch, Peter, you will go to the barn and smokehouse. Find out how much food we have stored. Crops are starting to suffer. We'll take as much as we can, and leave the rest for our neighbors."

"Why?" Peter sneered. "They're not doing anything for us."

He received such a glare that he went silent and only nodded. Papa had been keeping him overly busy lately. Anna thought at first that checking the food supply was just another way to keep Peter out of trouble. But then the subject of food shortage came up again during the meal.

"Anna," Mama said as she wrapped her own bun in her napkin, "for now, I think it would be wise to prepare the soup with more water and less potato. And let's try to manage with fewer buns."

"Why, Mama?" Susie protested, clutching her bun protectively.

"We may be facing a famine this summer," Papa answered. "With the heat and the armies trampling fields and needing our food, Mama is just taking precautions."

"The good news," Mama said, cheerfully, "is that we will eat with the elderly at the seniors' home, and they often have the best crops of all."

"Good news," Anna mumbled, and Susie leaned back in her chair to pout.

Papa turned to Anna. The subject of her money pouch hadn't come up since that day in the kitchen. He had never even asked for the money back. But she had never taken any more either. "There is good news for you, too, my dear," he said. "I have offered your services at the seniors' home as a worker. You will be given odd jobs and paid a little for them. You can keep some of the money that you earn for your pouch. You may earn us all a trip to Canada."

Anna's eyes brightened. "Really, Papa? May I?"

Mama laughed. "If only you would show the same enthusiasm for the work I give you."

"Perhaps if there was money."

Papa shook his head but smiled. "Your love for money will hurt you someday," he warned.

"It's not my love for money, Papa. It's my love for freedom.

For a land where we can eat cake and live without war."

"You just want to see your boyfriend," Peter mocked. Anna turned her nose up at him but smiled just a bit.

"I want cake," Henry stated with his mouth full of bun.

"And someday you shall have it," she promised her little brother.

"Lord willing," Papa and Mama said together. And for the first time in weeks, the whole family smiled all at once. Even Peter's eyes lit up at the thought of cake. Maybe things would be all right.

With only two more weeks until the move to the seniors' home, the whole family worked diligently to prepare. Even the news that traveled around the colonies seemed to flit right past them in their busyness. Only Peter seemed to care about the world outside their busy home.

"Do you know the Makhnovtsky have been burning and looting nearby villages?" Peter asked Anna one day as they washed the outside of the windows. "The fields are being trampled and destroyed too. That's why Mama and Papa don't want us to eat so much."

"That can't be true," Anna said. "Makhno is in the Khortitsa settlement. Besides, we would have heard if they were close."

"Where from?" Peter asked. "Papa won't talk about him and you've hardly been out of the house. They've nearly destroyed the Khortitsa with lice and typhus and fire. Some of our men have even gone down to help. Now they're coming here."

Anna didn't want to think about Makhno and his band. It was bothersome enough dealing with the steamy heat that began at sunup and lasted late into the darkness.

"Who wants to be out of the house in this heat," she answered instead. She blew a wisp of limp hair out of her eyes and looked at the bucket of water she held. "Hey, Peter," she said. And when he looked up, she dumped the bucket over his sweaty head.

"Ahhhh!" he shrieked as he chased Anna with his own bucket. He cornered her outside the front door. "Now I'll wash away those silly sommersprossen dotting your face!" Peter tossed the rest of his dirty but coolish water at her summer freckles and all down the front of her dress.

"Children!" Mama came to the door in a fury. "What are you doing?!" Anna had never seen Mama so angry about a little harmless fun.

Anna and Peter looked at themselves, completely dripping, and couldn't stop smiling.

"Just keeping cool, Ma," Peter said.

"Don't you know how precious water is right now?"

"Sorry," Peter offered, and Anna nodded.

Mama shook her head. "I'm sorry too," she said. "You just don't understand."

"Is it that bad?" Peter asked.

Mama sat on a stump and nodded. "The crops are drying up. We have to use water wisely. There's no way to know when it will rain again."

"But the river still has water," Peter insisted.

"Not enough, and it's not so easy to get it to the crops," Mama sighed. "That, too, will dry up someday."

"Maybe we could offer to haul water for some of the farmers!" Anna said excitedly. "We could make some money!"

"There she goes again," Peter muttered. "Money, money, money."

"Freedom, freedom, freedom," Anna answered back. Peter probably would have retorted about freedom in Russia, but their banter was halted by a group of kids running through the streets.

"Fire!" they called wildly. "Fire down the village!" Anna and Peter ran into the street to see where they had come from. Sure enough, dark spirals of smoke lifted into the air from the other end of the village.

"Makhno." Peter barely breathed the word. Then, in a voice filled with terror another name escaped: "Hildi!"

"I'm gonna help!" he called as he picked up his bucket and grabbed Anna's out of her hand. He ran toward the burning end of town.

Anna raced back to the house where Mama stood. "What should we do?" she asked.

"You stay here with the children," Mama replied after a moment. "In this dry heat, the fire will spread. If it comes as far as the church, move the children out into the street."

The church! That was only three doors away. Could it destroy them all?

"What about all our stuff?" Anna stammered.

"Leave it. Susie can keep the children outside. You do what you can to help the neighbors."

Mama followed Peter and dozens of other villagers running toward the fire.

"Oh, God," Anna cried, clasping her hands together in desperation. "Keep them safe.

"Keep us all safe."

As Susie watched the children, Anna watched the road. Nobody was returning with news. Only mothers and young girls, like Anna, remained at this end of the village. After what seemed only minutes, Anna began to smell the smoke, and soon the sound of crackling and snapping sparks accompanied the smoke pillars and the glow of the fire. Along with the noise of the flames came the hollers and deep, desperate cries of those fighting it.

The church, only three buildings away from them, stood empty and quiet, as if it were just waiting to burn. Anna had seen her mother stop in there to get her father before disappearing down the road. Something seemed strange about her own papa leaving the church with a bucket in his hand.

Before long, the voices of the men were close enough to

make out their very words and then Anna saw the flames. They were so near now that Anna knew she had to take action. She saw a house on the other side of the church burst into flames. Only a few more before it reached the church.

Then Anna had a thought. Papa's Bible. That's what had seemed strange about Papa leaving the church. It wasn't that he carried an empty bucket; it was that he didn't carry his precious Bible. He never went anywhere without his Bible. It must still be in the church!

"Susie!" Anna called. "Get the children outside. I'm going to the church!" The air around the church was filled with choking smoke. She had to be quick. The old wood could burn quickly.

Anna swung the church doors open, and a blast of smoke, which had seeped in through the window, jumped out at her. Anna struggled through the smoke to the front of the church.

Papa's Bible had been passed down from his own father and it remained his most treasured earthly possession. Not all the villagers were lucky enough to have German Bibles, and Papa said it would soon be impossible to get them. As a pastor, it was very important for him to have one. For a second, Anna remembered that he wouldn't be the pastor of their village much longer, but the sad thought was interrupted by the welcome sight in front of her.

"There it is," she gasped as she lunged toward the front pew to rescue the Bible. She grabbed it and turned toward the door, almost stumbling over her own hurried feet. She burst outside as villagers surrounded the building.

"Anna!" her mother shrieked as Anna tumbled out of the smoky building, but the sound of shattering glass startled them both. They turned to see the flames, which had jumped from the other house, eating up their precious church.

The villagers were giving up. At the sight of the church burning, most of them scattered to their own homes to rescue their belongings. Mama followed her neighbors. "Never mind the house," she called to Anna. "Help the others." But Anna raced home with Papa's Bible in her hand. She saw Susie on the street with the children, some blankets, pots, and kitchen chairs.

There was just one more thing that Anna must save. She ran past her brothers and sisters into the house. Her pouch was no longer hiding, but sat on top of the fireplace. She stuffed it into her dress pocket, grabbed a few books and toys, then ran out to the street.

The house next to theirs was burning already. Anna noticed for the first time that the gap between their home and the others was larger than most. She wondered if the distance was great enough to stop the flaming sparks. She dropped to her knees and called out in a way she had never done. "Stop the fire, Lord! Use this wide space to stop the fire." As Anna prayed she didn't notice the noise in the street become quieter as people stopped. Some watched the fire. Some watched Anna.

Some joined her to pray. The gap wasn't so great that sparks didn't leap across, but as they landed on the clay roof that Papa had specially built, they fizzled out and the fire spread no further.

Chapter 9

Gypsies

When the fire stopped spreading, the yelling of the firefighters subsided also, and the streets took on a more mournful voice. Both crying and heart-felt praise filled the air, for the lives and houses that were lost and those that were saved. Anna and Susie herded the awe-struck children back into the house. Though most of the neighbors clung to one another or worked together clearing the belongings from the street, Mama stood alone and helpless, staring blankly at the others from her front porch.

"Shall we make supper, Mama?" Anna asked. Mama's cheeks were streaked with tears and ash. Her hair had tumbled out of its perfect bun and hung in damp wisps over her tired, glassy eyes.

Mama shook her head first, then nodded. "Whatever you like," she finally mumbled as she leaned against the doorpost, looking out at the tragedy-struck village.

Susie, who had been fighting back her own tears, asked, "Where are Papa and Peter?"

Mama shut her eyes and turned right into the doorpost, burying her face against the wood. "I don't know," she whispered in a cracking voice. "I don't know." At that moment baby Elizabeth cried and Anna turned to hush her.

As if suddenly remembering her role as mother, Mama stood herself up straight, smoothed her apron, pushed back her hair, and swallowed her tears. "Make supper, girls," she said a little too firmly. "We best get on with things." She picked up the baby and squeezed her until Elizabeth squirmed to get loose. Anna and Susie hurried to the oven, even though neither was hungry for the thin soup they were eating almost every night.

During supper, a stomping of boots outside startled Anna. She dropped a ladle as she turned to see her father and Peter at the door. Mama nearly dropped the wiggling baby as she raced into Papa's arms.

Peter staggered through the kitchen silently, as if in a trance, and went straight to the bedroom.

Mama watched him go and turned back to Papa. "What happened to you?" she wailed, almost angrily. "I never saw you come out of that big house. I thought you were dead!" That sent Susie into tears as she ran into Papa's arms too.

Anna still watched the bedroom door, wondering what had put such terror in Peter's eyes. Nothing frightened Peter. He was always the hero. Now he looked like the town's worst victim. Anna quietly sneaked past the others and tapped on the bedroom door. Peter stood at the window staring at the trees outside. A cloud of dingy, gray smoke hung over them, slowly dropping to seep between the branches and swirl around the trunks.

"Are you all right?" she asked. Obviously, he wasn't, but she knew no other way to begin. Peter lay his forehead against the window and groaned. "I know it must have been terrible, Peter. I watched it all. But you're alive. God protected you. And Papa. And even the house, Peter." Anna meant the words to encourage him. Perhaps this is what he needed to turn back to the Lord. She wasn't prepared for his response.

"Not all of us," he mumbled in a strangely dark voice. "Hildi is dead."

Anna gasped. No matter how much she hated Hildi, she had never imagined that would happen. Peter waved her away, unable to speak, so she left the room quietly. In the kitchen, Mama and Papa had sat down. Susie lay curled up in Papa's lap, and the babies played at his feet as though nothing unusual had happened.

"It was Makhno's band. Someone saw them." Papa said. "I heard the Voth's neighbors talking. The Voth's were hard on their servants, and some of the servants were sympathizers." He looked at the girls. "That means the servants supported Makhno's group. They probably set the whole thing up. He torched the house while they ate. The whole family died in the fire." Papa looked up to see Anna. "Anna, dear," he said sadly. "A young girl from your class lived in that home. She's gone now. I'm sure she must have been a friend of yours. Peter said he had known her."

"I know," Anna answered quietly. "But she wasn't really . . . I mean . . . we were never close." Tears welled in Anna's eyes and she rushed to Papa's side. It didn't seem the right time to tell him that Hildi was the same classmate who had been a part of Peter's accident. "Oh, Papa! I was never kind to her. I was awful. But Peter liked her. And now . . . oh, it's going to be awful. Peter will never forget this. He will never forgive Makhno or God. We will lose Peter to this war now. I'm sure of it."

Papa didn't say a word to Anna but pulled her close and said a short, quiet prayer for peace and protection. Anna wanted to fall asleep on Papa's shoulders, but the little ones began to cry out for their supper.

Anna and Susie rose slowly to get the supper on the table. The thought of eating made Anna feel ill, but she knew it was the best thing for everybody to stick to a routine.

"Should I call Peter?" Susie whispered to Anna.

"No," Anna warned her. "He'll come when he's ready." Although that may not be for a very long time, she thought to herself.

Supper was quiet as they all listened to the commotion outside. Some neighbors cried; others called their heart-wrenching blessings and offered help from down the street. It wasn't the normal sounds of the supper hour, but Anna was glad to have some kind of noise to drown out the silence in the home. She sensed that Papa belonged out there, helping and praying with the people, but the people didn't seem to want his help anymore. Anna ached for her father as he listened helplessly to the cries. Then, as though something had swept through the whole village, the noise outside stopped. Anna looked up after a moment and noticed Papa listening carefully too.

"Run to the window, Susie," he instructed.

Susie trudged instead and stood speechless when she got there. Papa rolled his eyes toward the window and said, "Anna," motioning for her to go look. What she saw stunned her.

"Papa! It's the gypsies! They're in the street. Right outside our house!"

Chapter 10

Peace and Forgiveness

Mama gasped, but Papa moved to the window as calmly as if he were checking for rain. What he saw made him shake his head. A group of gypsy men and women, about ten of them, stood in the streets, looking around for something or someone. Their clothes were old and worn, layered thickly, and mostly unmatching. Hats and scarves of different sorts covered the long black hair of both the men and the women. On their arms and their necks the women wore interesting collections of chains and bangles.

But it wasn't because of the gypsies or their unusual appearance that Papa shook his head. He shook his head at the villagers—their own people—who stood in nervous little clusters close to their homes. They all watched the gypsies in terror and disgust, crossing their arms and tilting their heads suspiciously as they whispered among themselves. But nobody came forward to talk to the gypsies.

Papa strode to the door, mumbling about silly rumors and crazy fears. Then he went straight out into the street and walked up to the gypsies. Mama, Susie, and Anna watched from the door. Anna couldn't hear them speaking, but watched them nod and shake hands.

"Do they speak German?" Susie asked in surprise. Only Mennonites spoke German in Russia.

"I doubt it," Mama said. "But Papa knows some Russian and Polish, remember?"

Anna smiled for the first time since Peter had dumped water on her early that day. "It wouldn't matter," she said proudly. "Papa speaks with his eyes and hands. Look. Everybody understands that." Papa motioned to a few of the other village men. After seeing Papa smile, they gladly came to join him in greeting the strange visitors. Few reached out to touch the strangers, but they all smiled and spoke kindly.

After a few more moments, the gypsies nodded and turned to leave. The men who had been speaking to them grinned among themselves and patted Papa on the back joyfully. Mama and the other wives ran out into the street to see what was happening.

"Stay here," Anna instructed Susie. "I want to go too."

"How come you always get to . . . ?" Susie's voice faded as Anna raced out to hear about the strange gypsies in their village.

"They'll return tomorrow to help rebuild," Papa was saying to the women who had joined them.

Mama, seeing Anna, came toward her. "Isn't it wonderful," she exclaimed with tears in her eyes. Anna had never seen her mother so emotional, but was relieved, at least, that the tears were accompanied by a smile this time.

Mama continued: "They will make a big rabbit stew for our supper tomorrow, and the men are going to help us rebuild! They even want to help with the church. Pagan's or not, they have hearts of gold. Oh, what a day this has turned out to be. We've had enough excitement to last a lifetime."

"Where are they going to get rabbit?" Anna asked. Her mouth almost watered at the thought.

"Oh, those gypsies have all sorts of strange tricks," Mama answered. "But let's not question the Lord." Arm in arm, Mama and Anna walked back to the house, where Susie waited anxiously with the crying children. Peter was at the window watching too, but before anybody had a chance to talk to him, he muttered something about talking to the gypsies and raced out the front door. Mama called after him, but he didn't appear to hear—or care.

Mama explained away his actions. "He's just upset. He's not talking sense. Just leave him."

As Anna watched him go, she saw Papa head toward the ruined church. She would have to let him go, for now, because she had other things to do. She ran to the cupboard where she had put the Bible.

"Can I go with Papa?" she asked and barely waited for Mama's silent nod. She could hear Susie in the background, complaining again about being left behind.

"Papa!" she called to him, but he was standing in the ash of the church, deep in thought. Heat still radiated from the stone parts of the structure that remained standing. Anna walked carefully to avoid tripping over chunks of rock and fallen, crumbling beams on the floor. The smell almost made her nauseated and the sight of their beloved church caused her to wince inwardly. Papa must feel ten times worse. This had been his church for so long. She walked up behind Papa and tapped him on the shoulder.

"Oh, hello," he said, turning to her. She held out the Bible and saw his eyes widen in surprise, then joy, and then shock. "You didn't come in here . . ." He couldn't bear to finish the sentence.

"It's okay, Papa. It was safe." Anna hoped that in all the bustle her mother had forgotten that she had seen her only seconds before the church went up in flames. "I couldn't bear for you not to have it."

Papa took Anna in his arms and hugged her for what seemed like hours. "You know a true treasure, Anna," he finally told her. "I don't know where I would have gotten another."

"Read something," Anna suggested. She needed to hear something to lift her spirits, but even more than that, she desperately wanted to hear her father's soothing voice, the way it always sounded when he read to her from his Bible.

Papa smiled as he opened the Bible, flipped the pages, and settled on a passage that he had read often. "'Thy word have I hid in my heart, that I might not sin against thee.' That verse may mean more than it ever has before, my dear." Papa spoke with a heavy heart. "The way this war is going, it is doubtful that we will have much freedom left."

"What else can they take?" Anna asked bitterly. They took away peace; they forbid speaking German in public places; they even took most of the village horses for the war.

"I don't believe that the Red Army—if they win—will be kind to our people. They are not so tolerant as the czar's government was. They may take our churches and our Bibles too." Papa turned to Anna, tucked his Bible under his arm, and grasped both of her hands in his.

"Promise me, Anna," he pleaded. "Learn God's Word now, while we still have it with us.

"They can take our Bibles, but they cannot wipe out our memory."

Anna nodded vigorously, then looked up to see most of the village men standing outside the church where the door used to be. It struck Anna as funny, that they should wait so politely at the door although there were no walls and barely a floor left.

"Pastor," one of them said, as they all picked their way through the ash and debris. Some of them cleared their throats and looked down at the floor, ashamed to look Papa in the eyes.

"Pastor," he said again. "We've been thinking. We know that we haven't been supportive of you lately, and we know you have plans to leave. We were hoping that you might consider staying. We need a good pastor like you here. Especially now, with the funerals to conduct and all the healing that needs to be done. Soul healing, we mean."

Anna's heart raced. Maybe they could stay now, after all.

Papa's words struck her heart like a knife. "I'm truly sorry, gentlemen," he began. "But my word's been given. And besides"—Papa swallowed hard—"much of that healing needs to be done in my own family." Anna knew he spoke of Peter. "And I can't help a troubled church until I take care of that matter. There are good men among you. I love you all and thank you for your forgiveness. One of you can be a fine shepherd to this flock of sheep." Papa's voice broke as he said it. Anna could sense the relief he felt at having been forgiven for his son's debt.

The men stood around, shaking Papa's hand warmly, but regretfully. Anna snuck out. She needed to find out where Peter had gone and, more importantly, why.

Gypsy Trail was only a five-minute walk from the church. When Anna reached it, she hesitated. The gypsies seemed so friendly when she saw them talking in the village, but here, in their own surroundings . . . Anna thought to turn around, but she wanted to see what Peter was doing. For the first time in her life, she took a step onto the trail that led to the gypsy camp. There were no sounds coming from within the trees. Maybe, she hoped, they hadn't come back here. Maybe Peter had just gone for a walk by himself.

Anna had almost turned home when she saw the crackle of a fire in the trees. Her stomach flip-flopped at the sight of flames again, and all the horrible feelings of the day flooded back, but she realized it was a small bonfire, and there was movement around it. Then she heard voices: broken German with bits of Russian and one clear, strong German voice. It was Peter. Anna froze and looked for a place to hide. Some of the trees were wide and she was small. Slowly, careful not to disturb the underbrush, she slid behind a large tree and listened.

"You must have some," Peter urged impatiently.

The gypsies shook their dark, covered heads. "No, no," they repeated, in broken German. "No guns."

"No, Peter," Anna moaned in her heart and turned to run home. Tears stung her eyes as she went, but when she saw the shell of the church and her house in the distance, she couldn't bear to go there. Instead she slipped into a grove of trees behind the church and dropped to the ground. There she curled her knees up under her chin and rocked, just the way she had done when she was a baby. The heavy, acrid smoke still hung in a fog around the trees. It felt thick in her throat and nose.

"Oh, God," she cried as she swallowed a mouthful of the gray smog, but no words would come. Instead she lay still and cried until she finally drifted into a deep, tired sleep beneath the trees.

Chapter 11

Changing Plans

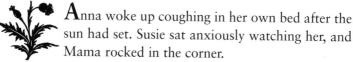 Anna woke up coughing in her own bed after the sun had set. Susie sat anxiously watching her, and Mama rocked in the corner.

"Mama!" Susie yelled so loudly that Anna almost fell out of the bed. Mama rushed to Anna's side.

"Oh, my baby," she cried. "Mama's here."

Anna sat up and wiped her eyes. "Peter?" was all she could think to say.

"He's gone for the doctor. He's the one that found you. Are you feeling all right? What happened?" Mama spoke so rapidly that Anna couldn't follow all her questions. Peter had gone for the doctor. That meant he had come home. Anna lay back against the cushions. It probably also meant that he hadn't found any guns. In her heart, Anna said a silent thank-you to God as she let her mother spoon soup into her mouth. After a bit of the warm, watery broth, Anna felt a little better, although the taste of smoke still stung her throat.

"I can get up," she assured Mama, but when she tried, she found her muscles ached with stiffness from sleeping on the hard dirt and rocks.

Papa came in as she was painfully trying to stand. He raced to her side and picked her up in his arms. Anna cringed as he squeezed her aching body. "I'm fine, Papa," she told him. "Just a little sore."

"You must tell us what happened," he insisted, but Anna

could tell by his voice that he feared the worst.

"I just fell asleep,"

"Nobody hurt you?"

"No, sir." Anna felt a little ashamed at having caused so much concern. She felt even worse at not being able to tell her Papa the truth, but he was so relieved to find out she was really all right that he didn't think, at that point, to ask any more questions.

But why shouldn't I tell Papa? Anna asked herself. She feared for Peter. She couldn't bear to think of what might happen if he found a gun. But if she told, there would be so many awful feelings and angry words. It may even drive Peter away for good. She argued with herself. She just couldn't bear for the family to be broken up. "Is that how strong Peter feels about protected us from the soldiers and the Makhnovtsky?" she suddenly thought. For the first time in weeks, she began to understand him.

Papa and Mama helped her to the sofa, and Susie carried her soup tray away. After they were all settled, Anna said, "I went to find Peter."

"And?" It wouldn't do to tell Papa she got lost. She knew the village woods as well as the rabbits.

"I guess I was just so tired from the fire. And the smoke made it hard to breathe." Anna finished as Peter and the doctor rushed through the door. At least she hadn't had to lie.

Mama jumped to get the doctor's hat and coat. "Oh, she's much better," Mama told him, but he insisted on examining Anna anyway. When he finished, he turned to Papa.

"I suppose it's just as well for all of you to hear this," he said with concern in his voice. "Anna was lucky. Lots of vagabond soldiers wandering about, and Makhno's men. Not many reports around here, mind you. Mostly in the old colony—Sagradovka and Nicolaipol. But it's not safe for young ones to be out alone. Just in case."

"Thank you, Sam." Papa shook the doctor's hand firmly.

"We will be cautious for our remaining time here."

"How long now until you go?"

Papa cleared his throat. "I haven't yet discussed it with my wife, or family," he said, "but in light of today's tragedies, I believe we'll go a little early. Perhaps the day after tomorrow. School's almost finished, anyway."

"Papa!" the three oldest children protested.

"Not so soon!" Susie pleaded.

The doctor slipped out then, with a quick good-bye to the family.

"Why?" Mama wanted to know. Even she looked a little disappointed in him. "Don't you want to help rebuild?"

"In a way, we are," Papa answered. "The Friesens down the way are too old to go through the rebuilding. Their hearts are nearly crushed at the loss already. If we go now they can have this house, and widow Janzen, who's also lost everything, has agreed to move in here with her two children to help care for them. I was just speaking to them all. I would like all of you to consider this. It has been a difficult decision, but I think it's what we must do."

"Won't there be enough money when you sell the house to emigrate?" Anna asked hopefully. It wasn't a big house, but she knew it must be worth something. Others had sold their homes to emigrate. That's how Johnny's family had managed it two years ago.

"Anna, love," Papa said. His face sagged from fatigue. "Nobody will pay us for this house. Everybody wants to sell, these days. Nobody wants to buy. If we don't give it to the Friesens, it will sit empty. Perhaps we can make some money from the cows, if they survive another week. Don't count on it."

Anna looked anxiously to Mama, hoping she might argue with Papa. Persuade him to try. It was their only hope. Once that was gone, they would own nothing of value. But Mama didn't even try. She just nodded and quietly said, "I'll begin packing." Then she turned to Peter. "Go get some crates from the barn."

Anna had dreamed many times of Mama saying those very words. But in her dream, she said them as Anna poured her pouchful of money onto the table. And in her dream they were packing for Canada, not for a seniors' home in a nearby village.

She shook herself out of her daydream and followed Peter through the hall to the attached barn. She meant to offer her help, maybe speak to him in the privacy of the barn, but Peter continued out the back door of the barn into the dark night. In the blackness, Anna could almost forget the direness of the day, or at least pretend it had only been a dream. Apart from the acrid smell of smoke still lingering, the village remained as peaceful and quiet as on any other warm summer night. For the first time Anna could remember, she desperately wished they didn't have to leave it.

When Peter heard her footsteps behind him, he turned. "What are you doing?" He sounded angry. "Didn't you hear what the doctor said? You shouldn't be alone outside at night."

"But you're here," she defended herself. "I'm not alone."

"What makes you think I can protect you?" Peter picked up a stone and hurled it at a fence post. "I'm only fifteen, remember? And I wasn't much good to Hildi, was I?" His voice ached with bitterness. "She's the only one that understood me. She was something special," he said, looking up only briefly to gauge Anna's reaction.

Anna was careful not to react at all.

Then he hung his head again. "And what good was I to her?" he asked.

"You can't blame yourself for that, Peter."

Peter picked up another stone, grinding it into the palm of his hand as he stared out into the dark street for a more satisfying target. Fortunately, the street was empty of people and animals. Maybe the doctor's warning had spread already and everybody was hiding inside. "You just don't understand what it's like being a man."

If Peter hadn't sounded so serious, Anna may have laughed. "Why can't you just be a kid again?" she asked instead.

"I just can't. I've seen too much. They killed Hildi." His voice choked. "And somehow," he said, suddenly filled with hateful anger again, "I'm going to kill them." Then he hurled the stone violently into the night, not caring what it might hit.

Anna cringed, half expecting to hear the howl of an injured animal when the stone finally landed. The night remained silent, however, until Anna whispered, "That's not how God wants you to be."

"Does God want us all to die in flames?"

"Of course not, but—"

"There are no arguments, Anna. Our people are dying all over this country and millions of good Russian people too. Someone has to stop it. I want to be the one."

"Where did all this hate come from?"

"It's the way of the world, little sister. Someday you'll understand."

"I hope not!" Anna called over her shoulder as she ran back to the house. "And don't ever call me your little sister again." She didn't say it loud enough for him to hear, but next time, she was sure, next time she would say more than she wanted to.

In the house, Mama and Susie had already begun wrapping dishes in towels and rags.

"Are the crates here?" Papa called from the bedroom, where he stood collecting his books and papers. Anna went straight to him. "Oh, Papa," she cried. "You have to do something about Peter."

"Shhh." Papa hushed her as he shut the bedroom door

quietly. He came and took her hands in his. "I know all about Peter, Anna," he soothed her. "That is partly why we are leaving sooner than planned. Anna, can you keep a secret?"

Anna nodded.

"Jacob Penner's group is back." Papa said. "Peter mustn't know that."

"What can I do?"

"Don't tell anyone—not even your mother. And pray."

"Yes, Papa," Anna sighed. "I wish I could do more."

"More? Anna, what could possibly be more helpful than prayer. Putting Peter's safety in the Lord's hands is like . . ." Papa thought for a moment. "Well, it's like sewing your leather pouch of money to your heart. God cares for Peter more than you care for that money, and he will keep Peter as close to him as he can.

"That reminds me," Papa said as he reached into his pocket for a shiny coin. "Somebody gave this to me today and I thought you should have it for your pouch."

"Thank you, Papa." Anna smiled. She hadn't been able to add to her pouch since that day at the market.

"There is one more thing you can do, Anna," Papa added hesitantly. "I hate to ask it of you, but . . ." Papa hesitated. Anna could tell he was going to ask something that went against his ideals. "Will you watch Peter and let me know if anything strange happens?"

Anna nodded. "Don't feel bad about asking, Papa. I know it's for his own good. Besides, I've been watching him, anyway, before you asked."

Papa smiled in a sad sort of way. "You're a good girl," he said. "And Anna, we will get there someday. To Canada, I mean. All of us."

"Peter too?"

"Peter too," Papa promised. Anna felt comforted by Papa's confidence, but deep down she knew he couldn't really make that promise. Only God knew for sure if Peter would be with them, and so far, God wasn't giving her any reason to think he might.

Chapter 12

Good-byes and Hellos

The following Monday the children went to school for the morning only. "Just to say good-bye to your teacher and friends," Papa reminded them.

Anna insisted on walking with Peter to school, despite his unveiled pokes about her being a nuisance. She kept an extra-close eye on him and prayed silently almost the whole way there. When a few of his Russian friends stopped him on the way to school, Anna stayed by his side, hurrying him along. She couldn't be too sure which of his friends were planning with him. She hoped Willie was no longer one of them.

"Why are you being such a pesky flea?" Peter asked after she sped him past a group of boys, tossing balls in the street.

Anna shrugged. "I don't want to leave with a tardy mark on my record," she lied.

Peter's silent acceptance of such a lame excuse gave her courage to add her true feelings. "It's hard to say good-bye, isn't it?"

Peter nodded. "And you want to go all the way to Canada?" he asked. The usual bitterness in his voice was gone. "That's a whole lot farther, you know."

"It's different," she replied. "It's easy to give up a little for a lot. It's much harder to give up everything for nothing."

Peter shrugged, and Anna wondered if he even realized that he was the reason they had to leave. Anna fought back the urge to tell him. "Can I walk home with you too?" she asked.

"We could toss rocks at the old stump the way we used to. It'll be the last time."

Peter smiled. "You never could hit the stump anyhow."

"Well, then I think I deserve one more chance."

"All right, but you'd better be ready as soon as lunch starts."

Anna nodded enthusiastically and ran to her friends on the swings. She hadn't realized how badly she had wanted him to agree—to accept her company without complaint. When she said it, she had meant it only as a means of keeping an eye on him, but she was thrilled that he had agreed. Saying good-bye would be hard, but at least she had her brother back! Things would be all right.

Neighbors had wagons at the house at sunrise to help carry the family's belongings to the seniors' home. It was going to be another hot, dry day, and Anna was grateful they were leaving early. As she helped load dishes and clothing onto the wagons, she heard bits of talk between the men.

"Things getting worse, I hear . . ."

"Be better to be out of the country if they win this war."

"Communists won't let us worship our way."

Anna tried to listen, but kept being jostled and shoved as the adults packed the waiting wagons. She had heard bits of it at school too, and she couldn't put it out of her mind. If the Reds—the Communists—won this war, things would change a lot in Russia, even here in the Molotschna, where they should be safe from persecution. The first sign of it came during Anna's last week of school, when the teacher began loading them with Bible memory verses. "Learn them now," the teacher warned, just as Papa had in the ashes of the church. "Bibles may become very scarce soon."

"Hey, Anna!" Margaret dashed down the street, waving to

her. "You weren't going to leave without saying good-bye, were you?"

"Of course not." Anna smiled and put down the crate of towels she held. "Papa was going to stop by your house on the way out if you didn't show up. I knew you would though."

"And with a surprise," Margaret said excitedly, waving an envelope. "I went to the post office, yesterday, when Mrs. Kroeker was sorting the mail. She mentioned she had something for you." Margaret handed her the envelope.

"It's from Johnny!" Anna shrieked and tore it open. She sat on the edge of the crate and read it quietly to herself.

Dear Anna,
Where are you and why are you not here? I expected you to be here a year ago. I hear from my aunt that things are very bad in Russia. You must hurry or I should begin training a new business partner. I am only teasing, silly girl. I know you must be near tears over that. Come soon. I have something that I cannot tell you in a letter. I wish you would hurry up.
Love Johnny

As she read his words, Anna could hear his voice, although not as clearly as she used to. The handwriting, too, seemed different, and Anna had to close her eyes and imagine him before the words really became his. She flipped the page over to find more, but those were the only thoughts scribbled on the entire page.

"Anna?!"

Anna jumped and looked from the paper into Margaret's questioning eyes.

"Wake up, would you?" Margaret said, shaking her head, but not without a slight smile. "I want to know what he has to say?" she said. "Unless it's too mushy to share."

"I'm sorry," Anna apologized. "He says . . . um," Anna

looked down at the paper again and fingered it carefully. She swallowed a lump. "Only that he wants me to hurry and come there," she said quickly, trying to blink away any hint of moisture in her eyes.

His words had wrapped around her, feeling as though they would choke her. How long would he truly wait? Who had he met? What if he had found a girlfriend? Or maybe he really did find someone else to make plans with. And what couldn't he tell her?

She tucked the letter into her apron, cleared her throat, and picked up the crate again. "I'll write back from our new home," she mumbled to Margaret. "I'll send your love too."

Margaret nodded as Anna's father announced that they must now leave. Hugs and kisses rippled through the crowd. Margaret squeezed Anna tightly and both their eyes filled with tears.

"I'll visit," Anna promised as she climbed into the wagon, busily adjusting her skirts so she wouldn't have to look at anybody else. At last, the neighbors backed away from the wagon and they slowly began to move away from the house. Anna sat in the front of the wagon with Papa for the drive.

After a few minutes out of town, she told him, "I'm glad you're not going to be a pastor anymore."

"Why is that?" Papa asked, paying closer attention to the bumpy road and the wagons ahead than to what she was really saying.

"Because the Red Army doesn't like pastors."

Papa turned to her then. "Who told you that?"

"Lots of people," she said. "They said some of the Russian pastors and priests have been killed."

"You are getting too old," Papa told her, but he didn't say the words she most wanted to hear. She had hoped he would tell her that it was lies and everything would be fine. At that moment, they passed the burned-out home where Hildi had lived, and Anna knew things weren't fine at all. Even the fancy motorcar in the Voth's driveway had been destroyed. Both Anna and Papa looked back at Peter in the wagon and were relieved to see that he was asleep.

"When can we go to Canada?" Anna sighed.

"Soon," Papa answered. "As soon as the Lord provides a way."

Anna thought with some joy about the money she would be making soon, but she wondered if she could earn it fast enough. Things were changing much too quickly, and she secretly wondered if the time would come when they wouldn't be able to leave—with or without her money. At last, she fell asleep on Papa's shoulder and dreamed of the land of freedom until the wagons pulled into the yard of the seniors' home.

Chapter 13

Mrs. Reimer's Letters

Susie and Henry scrambled out of the wagon and Peter climbed down next with Elizabeth on his shoulders. Mama began unloading the wagon immediately. Anna knew busyness helped Mama forget her worries and sadness and thought maybe she would try it too. She took a box and followed Mama to the front door.

At the door, they were met by a large, grinning woman with a straight back and silver curls peeping out from under a brightly colored scarf. Her rosy cheeks seemed to erase some of the wrinkles in her worn face, and the power in her eyes stopped the entire family at the door. Anna took a second look, trying not to stare at this overwhelming woman. She was nothing like the weak elderly people Anna had imagined.

"Oh, how glad we are that you've come!" the woman exclaimed, grasping both of Mama's hands with her own large, tanned ones. "And such lovely children. Tell me, child," she stood tall, fixed her strong-looking fists on her wide hips, and looked into Susie's eyes. Anna could see Susie cower a little. "Can you read very well?" she asked.

Susie stared with her mouth gaping open until Anna nudged her. Susie managed to stutter, "Yes, ma'am. A little, I mean. But Anna reads so much better than me."

She turned then to Anna. "Well then, I have a job for you."

Anna's eyes lit up. Her first job!

The lady continued. "This daughter of mine—flighty

thing—can't stay put where she belongs," she began. "Well, anyway, she followed her dreams—or some such nonsense—to Canada, a place called Duchess, Alberta, I think, like so many are doing. She writes me ever so many lovely letters.

"Can't complain about that, mind you," she continued. "Many don't write once they're gone." She nodded secretively toward another woman, sitting in the corner, watching the scene, then went on. "But my Violet writes lots of pretty letters, and I don't have an ounce of strength left in my eyes with which to read them."

"I can read them to you," Anna quickly interrupted. She could barely hold her tongue and listen after hearing the words Duchess, Alberta. Her heart did a jig in her chest and she had to take a deep breath to settle it. Duchess, Alberta, was the city Johnny was living in!

"Fine, then. It's a deal. Come find me when you have a moment. I'm Mrs. Reimer."

Anna nodded, and Mrs. Reimer scurried away to tell the others about her luck.

Anna danced through the rest of the day and by afternoon finally found a moment to slip away to Mrs. Reimer's room. She tapped at the door, hardly able to stand still. She fixed her braids and rubbed her hands nervously while she waited for the door to open. At last, Mrs. Reimer swung the door and stood in front of her. How could such a strong lady have no strength in her eyes, Anna wondered. But she didn't dare ask.

"Come in, child." Mrs. Reimer motioned her to a small writing table. A stack of letters waited for her. They were very worn, and Anna guessed they had been looked at and held, if not read, many times already.

Anna began at the top. Mrs. Reimer said over and over what a lovely reading voice she had and how enthusiastically she read. Anna didn't tell her the real reason behind her enthusiasm, but she read every line, imagining that maybe, just maybe, Violet might mention a handsome young boy named Johnny she had just happened to meet. Anna knew, deep down, how unlikely it was, but she clung to the hope. If nothing else, she hoped to learn more about the city that would someday be hers.

After Anna had read until her throat was parched and scratchy, Mrs. Riemer stood and opened a large cabinet beside her bed. "And now," she said with a sneaky smile, "for your reward." She pulled out a brightly colored tin and opened the lid. Inside were ten round chocolate candies. Anna had never seen such rich-looking sweets. Not even the ones from Johnny's uncle had been this pretty. Mrs. Reimer held the tin out to her. "An old love of mine sends them every once in a while," she explained and blushed a little. "We were very young sweethearts. It didn't work out. We both married someone else eventually. Ever since my dear husband passed away, my old sweetheart has faithfully sent these treats. But he never comes himself. Haven't seen him in forty years."

"Oh, how romantic," Anna sighed.

"Romantic? Don't be ridiculous! Romantic would be if he would just come and sweep me off my feet, or at least send a letter with them. But I suppose he has his reasons. He's rich too." Mrs. Reimer sighed. "And I would have been, myself, if I had I married him, the way I wanted. But for now, I can only eat candy and pretend." She sat up straight and cleared her throat. "That will be enough for today. But perhaps tomorrow you can help me write back to her."

Anna nodded enthusiastically. That would be her chance. She could ask Violet directly about Johnny. Maybe Violet could be Anna's secret spy!

"Let's go," Mrs. Reimer said. "Dinner will be served soon."

"Dinner!" Anna bolted up. "I'm supposed to help with dinner. I have to go quickly."

"Yes, you must," she agreed. "But I wouldn't worry too

much. All that's going to be served is little wee buns and cabbage soup, if indeed you can call it soup. Someday"—she got a dreamy look in her eyes—"when this famine is done, I'm going to sit and eat twelve big buns all at once . . . with watermelon syrup. Wouldn't that be fun?"

Anna's tummy grumbled as she nodded. She had never had twelve buns at once.

"Come then. Let's go to the kitchen." Mrs. Reimer took her by the hand and led her down the creaky stairs. Although the white paint on the banisters was peeling and the faded wallpaper was crinkled with age, Anna had a good feeling about this new home. The evening sun through the lace curtains cast a speckled mosaic on the stairwell, softening the run-down appearance of her new surroundings and boosting the feeling of hope even further.

Mrs. Reimer had been right about the supper. There wasn't much to it, but Mama kept Anna busy scooping out soup and handing bun halves to all their new "neighbors." When Anna finally had a chance to sit at the small table set aside for her and the other children, she couldn't forget the words of Mrs. Reimer. A feast of buns would be heavenly, she thought, but with this famine it may never happen. Anna looked around the elderly people, some so thin already. It made her feel sick to think that her own family might end up starving to that size. But she wouldn't let it happen. She would get them to Canada before that ever happened. She would find new ways to earn money. Then Anna had a thought—if she could save money to help her family, Anna decided, she could start saving buns too. Then if thing got bad, she'd have food for her family. And if things didn't get bad, she and Mrs. Reimer could have that feast! As the others gobbled their little bits of food, she carefully wrapped her half bun in a napkin and slipped it into her pocket.

"Susie," she whispered. Susie looked up, with half the bun

already in her mouth. "Maybe you should save that."

Susie whisked the bun out of Anna's reach. "I'm hungry for it now," she insisted and looked at Anna as though she were out of her mind.

Anna sighed. She would have to do it alone—just like everything else. Later she placed her bun under a scarf in the one drawer that belonged only to her. In a week, she guessed, she would have seven. Anna calculated in her head. In two weeks it would be fourteen, if she could wait that long!

Anna slept with her pouch under her mattress again. Not as a way to hide it anymore, but because she thought it might help her dream of Canada. Once her eyes closed, however, even her dream world couldn't pierce her exhaustion. Then morning dawned and Anna sensed instantly that something wasn't right.

Chapter 14

A New Peter

Anna rolled out of bed and stared for a moment at the unfamiliar place in which she slept. Even after remembering her new home, she still felt a strange, eerie sensation. Mama was dressing the little ones in the corner, and Susie was still asleep. Papa was gone, but that wasn't so strange. Anna remembered that he would be leaving early to get some medical supplies from the hospital in the next village.

But Peter wasn't there. Anna bolted up. In all the excitement yesterday, she had completely forgotten to watch Peter.

"Where's Peter?" she asked in a shaky voice.

"He got up early," Mama told her. "I guess he's gone to milk the cows."

Anna glanced out the window. The sun wasn't shining, and she tried to tell herself that the gloomy sky produced this strange feeling she had. She noticed then that the cow barn stood just across a small field. There was no sign of anybody near there.

"I'm gonna go help him," she mumbled as she pulled on her dress and worn-out shoes. She bolted out the door and raced across the field. One of the men from the home was there, and from the deep droning fuss that the cows were making, Anna knew they had not been milked.

"Have you seen my brother?" Anna asked the man.

"No, little lady, but I sure hope he gets here soon, or I'll have to milk these beasts myself, and I'm just not sure they would like that any better than I would."

Anna raced back to the house, nearly knocking over Mrs. Reimer in the doorway.

"Slow down, child. There's no cause for running around here, unless that old barn is on fire or someone's handing out chocolate. And last I checked there was no such excitement."

"Have you seen my brother, ma'am?" she puffed, holding her side to stop the cramp that stabbed her there.

"Not today," she answered.

"My father?"

She nodded. "He left a couple of hours ago. Said he'd be back by ten."

"Do you know what time is it now?" Anna asked.

"Can't you tell time by the sun, girl? What do they teach kids, these days?" Mrs. Reimer shook her head and steered Anna toward the window. "Well, the clouds are thicker than I've seen them for a while, but you can still tell by the brightness that the sun rests right about there." She pointed up and then looked at Anna, waiting for a guess.

Anna shook her head impatiently. "I don't know," she said.

"It's just past nine thirty. Your father should be back soon."

"Thank you." Anna hurried back out to the front of the house. She stood in the center of the yard, scanning every corner for a sign of her brother, while watching impatiently for her father's buggy to appear down the drive. Every movement caused her to jump. None of the movements turned out to be Peter or Papa, though.

After a few minutes, Susie came running out. "Do you know where Peter is?" Susie asked hurriedly. "Mama's fit to be tied, she's so angry at him for running off without doing his chores."

"I don't know, but . . ." Anna hesitated. She wondered if

she should tell Susie her concern. She had promised to be silent about it, and Susie couldn't keep a secret for anything. But they may be wasting precious time if Peter had truly run away.

"Well, if you see him," Susie said. "You'd better warn him that Mama's awful angry. He wore his new boots out too. He's going to be in a whole lot of trouble." Then Susie disappeared.

Peter wouldn't need new boots if he was just messing around the farm. He would only need them if he had somewhere important to go—or if he needed them to last a long time.

"Don't panic yet," Anna told herself. "There's no reason to believe the worst." She thought back to yesterday. Peter had sat with them at supper and eaten quietly. She did notice him listening to talk at the table next to them. Three elderly men were discussing the war, just like all the men in the Molotchna settlement seemed to be doing. Suddenly, Anna's heart leaped. She had heard the name Makhno mentioned just as she was handing out buns.

"Oh, Anna!" she scolded herself. "You were so caught up in your thoughts of buns that you missed the most important conversation." If they had given any indication where Makhno was, that is probably where Peter has gone. She would have to find those men. Anna went looking through the kitchen first. Breakfast was still on the table for late risers, but Anna had no appetite. Only three ladies sat at the tables. Anna moved to the patio outside, where many of the men were sitting. Two were caught up in a game of checkers; one sat still and stared at the sun through squinty eyes; and a few more whittled bits of old wood. Anna knew right away that it would be hopeless to find the right men. She hadn't taken a close look at their faces, and they all looked so similar in every other way. Their hair was gray or almost gone in most cases, and all their skin was pale and wrinkly. She could never pick out the men who had been speaking of Makhno.

"Excuse me," she finally said quietly to the man watching the sky. "Have you heard the name of Makhno?"

His eyes opened wide and a strange fearful look came over his face before he stood up and limped, as quickly as he could, back into the home, glaring back at her once before disappearing.

Anna didn't know whether to run after him and apologize or leave him and not mention it again. She didn't dare ask anyone else. Some of them watched her nervously, as though hoping she wouldn't approach them.

Anna was called into the kitchen then to help clean up breakfast and could only shake her head when Mama asked if she had seen Peter. "That boy!" Mama complained. "He's going to have some explaining to do when his Papa gets here."

"Maybe he went with Papa?" Anna said hopefully.

"No, I saw Papa off myself. Peter is likely off exploring this new town. He's going to get himself a whipping when he gets back. He's not too big for that yet."

Anna wanted to beg Mama not to speak badly of Peter, fearing she may regret it very soon. But she had promised not to worry Mama about Peter, and there was nothing she could do anyhow. Nothing except pray; Papa's words came back to her.

"You know where he is, Lord," Anna whispered. "Keep him safe, and don't let him do anything foolish." Anna waited anxiously as the clock struck eleven, then noon. She tried to concentrate on the mundane jobs Mama kept sending her to do, but nothing could steer her thoughts away from Peter. Not until after lunch did she hear the rattling wheels of her father's buggy roll into the yard.

Some of the residents glared at Papa's loud and fast intrusion, but he seemed not to notice their irritated looks. He jumped quickly out of the wagon and practically dragged Peter down.

Peter wrenched his arm away from Papa, but leaned on his shoulder as he limped toward the house, cringing in pain with every step. Anna could see his ankle was swollen and his face looked hard and angry, but she didn't have a chance to ask why. The moment Papa entered the door he began barking orders.

"Everyone into the basement!" he hollered to the people on the patio and again when he got into the house. Then he turned to Anna. His eyes were flaming. "Where are the others?"

Anna ran up the stairs to the room where the babies were sleeping. Susie sat sewing while she watched them. "Grab Lizzy!" Anna ordered her sister as she herself grabbed Henry, squirming and yelling, off the mat on the floor. They could hear Papa yelling to the residents of the home and Susie, for once, obeyed without question and quickly trailed after Anna into the basement, where the others were gathering. Only Papa was missing. Everyone talked at once until Papa ran in, supporting an elderly lady with cane, and slammed the door.

Mama ran to him. "What is happening?" she begged as she eased the lady off his arm and offered her a nearly empty crate of potatoes to sit on.

All ears listened. "They're bombing villages. The hospital . . . air raids." Papa breathlessly tried to explain. "With clouds so thick, nobody saw it coming until the Red Army was right above. Bombed the hospital and half the village. They've been hitting different villages all morning." Papa stopped to take a breath and then muttered, "There's no reason why they might not come here next."

Before anybody could grasp his words, the sound of airplanes hummed above them. People cried, and prayed, and clung to each other in fright. Papa gathered his family together into a corner. For a few moments, nobody spoke.

Then, without warning, a nearby blast shook the building, and the basement went deathly silent.

Everyone crowded closer together in the dim candlelight, waiting and listening almost breathlessly. An occasional shuffle and the soft whimpering of Henry and Elizabeth, were the only sounds. Suddenly, two more blasts, one right after the other, shook the building. A few panicked voices shrieked, then went silent again to listen. Anna huddled closer to her family and buried her head deeper into her knees.

She didn't look up until she heard sniffling sounds beside her. Peter's head hung low, but his shoulders shook with sobs. When he looked up, his face was filled with terror.

"I don't want to die, Papa," he wailed. "I'm not ready!"

Papa put an arm around Peter, and for a brief moment the bombing stopped. "Don't tell me, son," he said warmly. "Tell God." Peter looked up and, for the first time in months, Anna saw her old, beloved Peter, without the hatred etched in his face.

"I'm sorry," he finally whispered in a choking voice. "Forgive me for everything. And save us please." Those were the only words he could get out.

Papa finished. "And help this child to forgive his enemies in the same way."

Another blast, the biggest of them all, fell at that moment. Anna buried her head in her mother's lap. Susie and the babies began to cry, and slowly others joined in. But Peter, Anna noticed when she peeked up, was glowing with joy.

No more bombs fell that day. After a few hours in the basement, Papa felt they could safely go back upstairs.

Chapter 15

The Feast

They stepped into the living area of the home cautiously. Before letting the seniors back into their rooms, Papa searched the building for fire, fallen beams and other fallout from the attack. Broken glass from blown-out windows was sprinkled over the floors of every room. Some shattered dishes lay under the tables, most of the picture frames had fallen off the wall, and a large antique vase that held umbrellas by the front door had tipped and cracked too. Anna and Susie helped Mrs. Reimer get the older and frailer seniors to their rooms for a rest and then began the daunting task of cleaning.

As Anna worked, sweeping glass and hanging curtains in front of the open windows, Peter limped up behind and startled her.

"I'm sorry," he chuckled as she jumped. "I didn't mean to scare you."

"That's okay." Anna answered warmly. "It's not the first time you've scared me. It's not even the first time, today, in fact." She noticed his ankle was bandaged tightly, and he walked with a cane.

"I'm sorry for that too. Actually, I'm sorry for a lot of things," he continued shamefaced. "I know you really tried to help."

"What happened today?" Anna asked him. "Before the bombing, I mean. I was frightened when I couldn't find you."

Peter looked away out the glassless window to the gray sky, and jammed his hands into his pockets. "God gave me a good sister," he mumbled, then slowly turned back to face her. "You did well to worry. I was gone to join Jacob and his group."

Although Anna suspected something like that, she couldn't help but gasp when the words were actually spoken. She turned and madly tried to scrub a gash out of the wooden sill as he spoke.

"But I fell into a hole and twisted my ankle," Peter continued. "Papa drove by on his way back from the hospital and found me trying to limp out. What crazy luck." Peter shook his head in disbelief.

"God was good to you. Was Papa angry?"

"No. That would have been easier." Peter sighed and slumped onto the floor beside Anna's pile of swept-up glass. He rested his forehead on his knees for a second then looked up. "Papa was so quiet and sad. Disappointed, I suppose. I don't ever want him to look at me like that again." Peter stood, pulled aside the curtain, and stared out into the fields dotted with pillars of smoke where small bombs had fallen. "I guess that's how God's been looking at me too, isn't it?"

Anna nodded, afraid to speak loudly in case tears spilled out. "I'm glad you're back," she finally whispered.

Peter had never liked mushy talks. "Hey, hurry up here and we can go toss rings out back."

"Not today, kids." They turned to see Papa smiling behind them. "There's plenty of cleaning up to do here." Papa handed Peter a hammer and a handful of nails. "Hope your foot won't interfere with the work of your hands," he said.

Peter shook his head. "No, sir," he muttered. "I figure I owe you all a lot of time and energy. I best get started now, or I'll never catch up."

Papa nodded his agreement and finished it off with a forgiving smile. "And Anna," he said, turning to her. "Mrs.

Reimer would like to see you. I told her you would come after you'd swept all the glass."

"Yes, Papa. I'm almost finished." Anna hurried to finish as Papa led Peter to another room. As soon as she had scraped up the last bits of glass and put them into the garbage bin, she ran up the creaky steps to Mrs. Reimer's room. The door stood open.

"There you are, child. I was starting to think that you wouldn't come, and then I would have to eat candy all by myself."

"Oh, it's been a wonderful day!" Anna bubbled.

Mrs. Reimer looked at her as though she had gone mad. "We were nearly blasted up to heaven today, child. Is that what you call wonderful? I'd hate to see what you call a bad day."

Anna laughed and explained to Mrs. Reimer all about her awful day and how it had ended so wonderfully with her brother.

Mrs. Reimer nodded knowingly. "I wondered what was going on in your corner of the basement," she said. "Well then, that is something to write about, isn't it?" She handed Anna a piece of paper and a pen.

"Sit down and begin like this . . ." Mrs. Reimer carefully relayed all the details that Anna had just given her. "So much more interesting that way, than just to say that we were bombed." After telling Violet all about Anna's joy, they told her about the chocolates and the weather, and about how the Red Army was getting stronger and the Mennonite people feared for their way of life. Then they each ate a chocolate. Anna was slowly addressing the envelope and was about to stuff the letter in when she got the courage to ask her question.

"Mrs. Reimer? May I . . . would you mind if I ask Violet one question? About a friend. He lives near her, I think." Anna fidgeted nervously. She didn't fear Mrs. Reimer saying no as much as she feared that Violet would tell her some bad news, or not tell her some good news at least. Anna told Mrs. Reimer about Johnny and their plans. "I just want to know."

Mrs. Reimer grinned and helped her write the questions on her heart and tuck the extra note into the envelope.

That night at supper, Anna saved another bun. Her stomach growled through the night, but thinking of her feast made it feel a little better, and the chocolates that Mrs. Reimer shared each day helped too.

The only news more important to Anna than news of Johnny came ten days after the bombing. "The war is over," people echoed in disbelief, but their voices were joyless. The Red Army had pushed the allied forces out. There was little hope now.

"What does that mean?" Susie asked Anna as they shared a bowl of weak porridge.

Anna thought before answering. "It means that things in Russia will change."

"They can't get much worse," Susie complained, scowling at her porridge. The cows weren't giving much milk now, because they were suffering from the famine too. "I heard that there won't even be cabbage in the soup tonight."

Anna already knew that. Mama had been up half the night trying to figure out how to make soup out of water and flour.

"The changes will be much more important than soup, Susie," Anna told her. "The Red Army—the Communists— don't like pastors, or churches, or Christians, at all."

"What will happen to us?"

"I don't know." Anna had lost her appetite talking about it. "You finish it," she said, pointing to the watery porridge. Only one person could take her mind off the war. She ran up the stairs to Mrs. Reimer's room.

"When do you suppose we'll hear back from Violet?" Anna asked. "Days still, dear," Mrs. Reimer sighed. It wasn't her usual high-spirited tone. She seemed distant. In her hand, she held tightly an envelope that Anna had not seen before. It looked fresh and new.

"Then that letter that you're holding isn't from her?"

"This? Oh no! This . . . oh, well, I guess I best let you read it. It's from him, I think."

"Your candyman?" Anna and Mrs. Reimer had always referred to her admirer that way. Anna wasn't sure she had ever even heard his real name. Mrs. Reimer smiled and handed her the letter. It seemed hard for her to let go of it.

Anna carefully opened it and began to read. "'My dearest Mary.'" Anna stopped reading and looked up. "I didn't know that was your name."

"Yes, yes, go on."

"'I hope you have enjoyed the gifts. I wish they could last forever, but I'm afraid they can't. My health has failed and I've lost my store. The armies cleaned out my shelves. I write not for your sympathy but for your forgiveness that I can no longer send you the gifts you have become accustomed to.'"

Anna looked up. Mrs. Reimer looked even more distant.

"He's a fool," she finally said.

"I beg your pardon?"

"A fool. To think that I would be more concerned about those silly chocolates than about his health. Well, at least he left a return address this time. What does it say? Where does he live?"

Anna read the last bit of the letter and the address on the envelope, which named a village many miles away in the distant Khortitsa settlement. Mrs. Reimer's face sagged in disappointment.

"It's too far."

"Too far to send a letter?" Anna asked.

"Too far to go. It would cost too much money. I haven't enough."

It hurt Anna to see such a strong lady so sad and helpless.

She knew that Mrs. Reimer was the one who had given her courage through these times. Anna searched her mind for some way to repay the favor, to cheer her friend up.

"Wait here," she instructed. Anna raced to her room and the drawer where she had been storing her buns. Ten days meant ten buns. Anna knew this was the time to share them. She would run to the kitchen for syrup too. Anna's mouth watered at the thought as she remembered the last time they had boiled watermelons for sweet syrup. Margaret and Willie had come to help too, and Anna was sure they had tasted more than they had saved. The only one who loved watermelon syrup more than Anna was Johnny. Someday soon she would get to share some with him again too. Anna pushed the memories aside as she excitedly opened the drawer and lifted the scarf and the clothing that covered her buns.

"Oh!" she gasped and covered her mouth. Her fresh white buns had turned dry and hard and green. Anna leaned over the drawer and cried. For ten days she had gone to bed with a hungry stomach, dreaming of a feast, and now the buns were wasted. How could she not have thought of mold? Even memories of syrup couldn't soothe her. When Anna's eyes ached from crying, she got up and dragged herself back to Mrs. Riemer's room. She sat on the floor, lay her head in Mrs. Reimer's lap, and began to sob.

"My dear. What can be so tragic?" Mrs. Reimer asked, patting her head.

"I had a feast," Anna wailed. When she had caught her breath, she explained the whole story to Mrs. Riemer. "And now it was all a waste," she finished, wiping the last tears from her eyes.

"It was a foolish thing to do," Mrs. Reimer agreed with a twitching smile. "A very foolish thing, indeed, but I wouldn't say it was completely a waste."

"Oh, how can you say that? Now I will have to throw all

those good buns in the garbage. Mama will never give me any more, and Papa will be so angry."

"Well, then you need to tell your Mama and Papa the important lesson you learned from this whole silly ordeal, don't you?"

Anna shook her head. "What lesson?"

"Don't you think that maybe you can learn something from this?"

"I learned that buns go moldy after time. But I suppose I already knew that; I just was too excited to think about it."

"That's not the lesson I was thinking of," Mrs. Reimer said, but still offered no suggestions.

Anna sighed deeply and thought. "I suppose I was being greedy," she answered, but she wasn't sure that was the right answer either. She had planned to share, and they were her buns, after all.

Mrs. Reimer said with a smile. "No. There's something more. Say the Lord's Prayer."

Anna began to quote. "Our father who art in heaven, hallowed be thy name. Thy kingdom come, thy will be done on Earth as it is in heaven. Give us this day, our daily bread—"

"Aha!"

Anna jumped out of her chair.

"That's the one! Stop there." Mrs. Reimer clasped her hands together proudly, as if she had written that prayer herself. "You did not trust God for your daily bread. You were saving up, just in case. And that, my dear, is where you went wrong. You see, God will take care of you—and he did. He made sure that you had a bun every day to keep your tummy full. You didn't accept that bread and trust God to keep your tummy full. You took matters into your own hands and started saving up, yourself."

"I thought I was being smart. It sounded like such a good idea when you said it."

"I said that someday I would have a feast, but not now, during a famine, dear . . ." Mrs. Reimer tried to finish her sentence, but she just started to laugh. "Oh, you are a fun child. So much like my Violet. She would have done just the same thing, no doubt." Then Mrs. Riemer sighed thoughtfully. "But what an awful day," she said. "I suppose you'd better go throw those buns out now."

"Yes, ma'am." Anna left the room thoughtfully. How could she not have thought of mold? Her mind had been so clouded with her dreams that she wasn't thinking clearly. Anna stopped suddenly in the hallway. That's exactly what Peter had said once about her money pouch. "You'll never save enough," he had told her. "But your head is so deep in the clouds you can't even figure that out."

Suddenly, visions of buns and coins mixed together in her mind, swirling and dancing, as though taunting her. Were they really so similar? Was saving money as foolish as saving buns? She was saving up for herself, and in the meantime, she was hoarding money that could be used for something else. She had even stolen from Mama's grocery money. Anna gasped quietly when the word stolen crossed her mind. She had convinced herself that it wasn't stealing, or at least she thought she had. But now it seemed the only word that fit. When Anna reached her room, she picked up her pouch. It was the heaviest it had ever been, weighted down by the coins she had earned here at the home. Peter still laughed and insisted that she didn't have nearly enough, but Papa said nothing.

Surely, if it were wrong to save, Papa would have said something. Wouldn't he?

Chapter 16

Anna's Greatest Sacrifice

"Mama!" Anna called down the hall to where her mother sat sewing. "Where is Papa?"

"He's out in the field, but you aren't to go out there."

"But I need to talk to him," Anna pleaded.

"It will have to wait. They've found unexploded shells out there. Your papa is checking the fields for more, and you are not to go near, do you understand?"

"Yes, Mama." Anna sat down on the bench next to her. "Do you think we'll ever go to Canada?" she asked.

"Yes dear, I do. Just as soon as the Lord provides a way."

"Is it wrong for us to save for it?"

Mama put her sewing down. "Saving and planning is never wrong," Mama said, and Anna breathed a sigh of relief. "If your heart is right," Mama added.

"What do you mean?"

"Well, you must always remember that it is God's money and not yours. That is the danger of saving. It is so easy to become fond of that money and forget that it belongs to God. Your papa believes in saving money, but it seems whenever he tries, the Lord asks him to give it to someone else. Do you remember our freedom jar?"

Of course Anna remembered; she would never forget. She nodded.

"Papa really felt that money should go to the soldier. He

didn't know why and he didn't ask. It was God's money. But you know something, darling. Every time God has asked for his money back, he has always provided another way." Mama began to laugh. "When you were a baby, we began saving for a pram for you. You were such a wiggly little thing that I couldn't carry you for very long. But then Aaron threw a ball through the Epp's window and broke it." Mama stopped for a moment. Anna knew she was slipping back in her memory to a time when her firstborn son still lived—a time before the logging camp. Anna waited patiently.

Mama took a deep breath and smiled again. "Well, anyway, we had to use that pram money to replace it. Winter was coming and it couldn't wait, you see. It took all the money we had saved. Not long after that, a Russian family came through town looking for a place to stay. We let them stay in our home for two days, and they noticed that I had nothing to push you around town in. They had a pram they were no longer using and it was far better than anything we could ever buy. They gave it to us to repay us, so we had a new window and a new pram. And new Russian friends too. That's how the Lord works, dear. He is always faithful. Does that make sense to you?"

"So you think God will provide the money for the trip without my help?"

"If that's his plan, he will."

"What if it's not his plan?" Anna's felt a lump of fear jumping in her stomach.

"Well, if it's not his plan for us to be there, do you really want to go? Do you want to sail for days on a boat that God doesn't want you on? Or try to live in foreign country without God's blessing?"

Anna shook her head. "But I want to see Johnny," she mumbled.

"God knows that, Anna. He will make you strong until

that day. Are you worried about your special savings?"
Mama asked.

Anna didn't have the voice to say anything.

"I'll tell you one thing," Mama said. "If you suspect that
God wants your savings for something else, you'd better give
it to him. It's the only way to keep it, really."

Anna nodded and got up to leave.

"One more thing, Anna," Mama said and lay her stitching
down. "Your papa knows you were angry when he gave away
our money to that soldier. He is waiting for you to understand."

"I do understand. That soldier needed the money, and it
wasn't ours to keep."

"Do you realize that if we had taken that money and left
the country a month ago, your brother may never have given
his life to God? God's plan is complex. Be grateful that your
father doesn't question it."

"I never thought of that." What if they had left before that
awful and wonderful day in the basement? Anna went back to
her room and pulled the pouch out from under her mattress.
She spilled the coins and counted them carefully. Peter was
right. It would never be enough for passage for seven people
to Canada. But it would buy a train ticket to the Khortitsa.

Anna dropped the coins back into the pouch and ran to
Mrs. Reimer's room. She lay sleeping on her bed.

"Goodness, child!" she shrieked when Anna burst through
her door. "Is it another bombing?" Mrs. Reimer leaped off
her bed and hastily began gathering letters, jewelry, and an
empty candybox.

Anna rushed to her bedside and spilled the coins onto the
bed. "This is for you," she told her with a smile. "To go take
care of your candyman."

Mrs. Reimer looked at her strangely. "Where did that come
from?"

"God," Anna answered. "Please take it."

Mrs. Reimer fingered the coins as though she held pure gold. "Why is it so important to you?" She sat on the edge of her bed and looked right into Anna's eager eyes.

"Because it's important to you. And besides, then you can thank him for me. For all the chocolates."

"How odd," Mrs. Reimer said, turning the coins over in her hand. "I had, just a moment ago, asked God for the money. I would have had it, you see, except that I sent a bunch in that last letter to Violet to take care of a medical bill."

Anna beamed. "That's how God works," she said proudly. "If you put your money where God wants it, he always gives it back when you need it."

"You are a smart girl," Mrs. Reimer praised her. "I guess it would be foolish of me not to take this."

"It sure would," Anna agreed. "That would ruin everything."

"Well, then, that only leaves one problem."

"Problem?" Anna had been sure everything would be fine now. And she didn't have any more money for extra problems.

"The problem of how I should ever manage in the Khortitsa without you. Or even more, how shall you manage here without me?"

Anna laughed. "Don't worry about me," she said. "If that is where God wants you, he'll take care of me here."

"God bless you, child," Mrs. Reimer whispered with tears in her eyes. Anna could only smile.

Chapter 17

Two Homecomings

One good-bye quickly led into another as Peter announced, shortly after Mrs. Riemer's happy departure, that he had plans too. One of the mills in their old village had been burned in the fire and the owner, Hildi's wealthy uncle, had asked Peter to come and help them rebuild it. He would pay him well, and it turned out that he too was a Christian man. Since Willie's family had agreed to take care of Peter, there didn't seem to be a good reason why he shouldn't go and help. Papa gave his permission, reluctantly admitting that Peter, almost sixteen years old now, was quickly becoming a young man of good sense. It wasn't until a week after he left that Anna understood why Papa had let him go so easily.

"We cannot eat their food any longer," Papa whispered to Mama on the patio under Anna's window one night. "There is barely enough food for the seniors."

"But what of our little ones?" Mama asked. She didn't question Papa very often, and it stirred up a whirlwind of worry in Anna's stomach. If Mama was challenging Papa's decisions, they must be desperate indeed.

"I still have my five-ruble gold coin," Papa reminded her. Anna sat up. She didn't know about any extra money. Perhaps it was the start to their trip. She leaned in to listen closer, full of sudden hope.

"I will take it tomorrow and see if I can get some food for

us," Papa continued, unaware of the heartbreak his words caused in the small bedroom of his children. "Now with Peter gone, it will be easier. I should get ten to fourteen pounds of millet for it. That is," Papa chuckled nervously, "if you can stand to eat kasha every day for a very long time."

"I'm sure I can make it as exciting as fried ham and borsht," Mama said cheerfully, although Anna guessed it wasn't real cheer. Mama loved to cook elegant food. "And even if I can't," she added, "plain kasha is better than gravel."

"How true," Papa agreed as they slipped away from the window and out of Anna's hearing. She sat for almost an hour in her bed, fighting back the tears. Why wouldn't Papa even try? If he was planning to spend his money on fifteen pounds of corn mush, that must mean he planned to stay for a long time.

"Oh, God," Anna cried out in her heart. "Why must we stay here? I have lost my best friends and my brother. My Papa is in danger now from the new rulers of Russia. What else will you take from me?" Anna buried her face in her knees, but the words in her heart were coming faster and stronger. "I am trying to understand. I truly am, but I don't. We will all die here and I will never see Johnny or Canada or any of my dreams!"

Anna began to sob uncontrollably. The tears poured down her cheeks and dripped onto her bare legs. When she finally had the strength to look up, she was staring into the brightest beam of moonlight that had ever filled her room. It seemed bright enough to light up all of Russia or even the world. *Maybe*, she thought, *Peter and Johnny and Mrs. Reimer were looking at the same moon and thinking of her too*. Somehow it made Anna feel closer to them and closer to God. She lay down on her bed, wiping the tears on her pillow. "I'll try to be patient," she said under her breath as she fell into a restless sleep.

When Anna woke the next morning, Papa was gone.

"He had to go for supplies," Mama said, and Anna knew it must be true then. She watched all morning as she cleaned the floors and windows of the center. The day seemed to drag until at last, just before supper, Papa returned home. He unloaded crates of packaged goods and asked Anna to help him unload. She peered carefully into each crate, looking for the hateful millet that would be their food for what seemed like the rest of her life, but none of the crates carried it. For a brief second, Anna's heart leaped. He's a change of mind! But then, seeing her father's stricken face, she knew that he had made no life-changing decisions.

"What's wrong, Papa?"

"I was hoping to get some food. There is none to be had in the area. Famine is cleaning out the entire country." His face looked years older from worry.

In her heart, Anna wanted to cry out that they should leave. That they needed to find a way to Canada, but the words that came out of her mouth sounded very different. "The Lord will take care of us, Papa," she reassured him in a quiet voice, then remembered her mother's words. "Papa?"

"Yes, darling?"

"I know you did the right thing when you gave that money to the soldier." She looked into Papa's face and the sagging wrinkles lifted a little as the corner of his mouth turned into a relieved smile. "And I know that God will give that money back to us." It didn't seem like the right time to tell him about her own sacrifice. From the look on his face, all that was needed now was a warm, forgiving hug.

"You are a grown-up young lady, all of a sudden," he said before letting go of her. "And you are right. We shall just wait. Since my money can't buy us food, maybe it will help us emigrate some day soon."

Although supper that night was flour and water soup, it

was a happy meal. The weight of hunger was lifted by the freedom of forgiveness and the power of hope. And it was made happier by Peter's entrance through the door, just as they were finishing.

"Peter!" Mama cried, running to hug him. Peter laughed and hugged back as the others circled him too. Even little Lizzy clung to his leg until he picked her up. "Why are you back so soon, and without warning?" Mama's voice was filled with joy, but touched with a bit of worry too. "We didn't expect you until Christmas."

Peter shoved his hands in his pockets and jiggled his knee nervously. "Well," he hesitated, "Mr. Voth had some family come to visit. Relatives from another city. They were having such a good time that Mr. Voth decided to quit work for a couple of days. And it just happened that another one of his workers was passing by this way, so he dropped me off for a . . . ," Peter cleared his throat, "a short visit."

"Oh, that's wonderful," Mama exclaimed, hugging him again. Anna looked at Papa, who watched Peter strangely, almost suspiciously, as though he suspected there might be more to Peter's story than he was sharing.

"Oh, but Peter," Mama wailed, "we have nothing much to serve you."

"That's okay!" Peter held up a finger signaling everyone to stay put and ran back to the door where he had hidden a sack. "This is for you." He grinned, handing Mama a crate of fresh eggs, a loaf of bread, and a package of smoked ham. "I had a good breakfast this morning."

"Where?" was all anyone could voice above the squeals.

"My boss, Mr. Voth, showed me his storehouse one day. He has enough food put away to last a ten-year famine, I think. I guess when the mill was doing well, he prepared for something like this. With the extra food, he is able to feed his livestock so he gets fresh eggs and milk too. Anyway, I asked if he could pay me, this week, in food instead of money, and this is what he gave me." Peter grinned from ear to ear as Susie and Mama continued to sniff and hug the ham.

"If you could do this every week, it would sure make it a lot easier to see you go!" Anna teased.

"Anna!" Papa scolded, but Peter only half smiled with a strange flicker in his eyes, then looked away from her and cleared his throat again. Again, Papa looked at him curiously, and smiled.

"So go ahead and eat." He shooed them all back to the table and sat down beside Anna. Although they had already prayed for this evening meal, it seemed important to thank God one extra time for this bounty. They all bowed their heads again before eating the delicious ham and bread. As the meal was being cleared, a loud voice echoed in the hallway and startled Anna. She listened closely.

"Just send that old desk to the room down the hall," ordered a familiar voice. "Goodness, child, can't you go any faster than that."

"Mrs. Reimer!" Anna pushed back her chair, knocking it right over, and raced down the hall to where Mrs. Reimer stood with her hands on her hips, surveying the building. Anna raced into her arms, and Mrs. Reimer squeezed her as though it had been years.

"You're back?" It was more of a question than a statement, but from the way the big lady was issuing orders, Anna suspected that she was there to stay.

"But what about your candyman?" she asked in a whisper before letting go of the hug.

"Why, I guess it's time you met the man, isn't it?" she said, just as a handsome elderly man walked out of her room. "This wonderful man is my new husband, Mr. Krahn. "And this," she said as she tugged at one of Anna's braids, "is the dearest child in the world."

Chapter 18

One Last Good-bye

Anna stared in disbelief. "You got married? That's great! But why are you here?"

"To say good-bye to you properly, my dear. But first, I must see your father. Is he here?"

Anna nodded and pointed toward the kitchen as her whole body filled with a disappointed ache. She wasn't staying after all. Without another word, Mrs. Reimer—no, Mrs. Krahn—and her new husband set off to find Anna's father. Anna slumped onto the stairs and began to cry. It would have been better if she hadn't come back at all. Two wonderful visits in one day only meant two more sad good-byes the next.

Ever since the day she had said good-bye to Johnny, she knew that good-bye was the hardest word in the world to say. It was harder than saying "I'm sorry" and harder even than those tricky Russian words they had to learn in school now. She wasn't ever going to say good-bye again. She would hide in her room when the time came, but she wouldn't say it.

When Anna heard the kitchen door open a few minutes later, and the mixed voices of Mrs. Reimer—Mrs. Krahn—and her parents, she scurried up the stairs to her room. She heard them call her, but she didn't budge. She would come out when they were gone, and not a moment before. The hollering stopped after a few minutes and was followed by a quiet knock on the door. Anna didn't answer, but her mama peeked her head in anyway.

"Mrs. Krahn would like to say good-bye to you, Anna."

"I don't want to say good-bye."

Mama smiled despite Anna's rudeness, but she wasn't going to give in.

"I think you need to listen to her."

Anna shook her head angrily as Mrs. Krahn herself stepped in the room, followed by Mama and Papa.

That wasn't fair at all. It was bad enough they were going to force her to say good-bye, but not with everyone watching too.

"May I sit?"

Anna nodded reluctantly, but wouldn't look up.

"You don't want to say good-bye?"

Again Anna shook her head, softly this time, while she stared at her feet.

"Well, I must say this isn't how I imagined it," Mrs. Krahn sighed and folded her hands in her lap. "Last time we talked you were so excited to go to Canada, and now you don't even want to leave. I'm flattered you want to stay in this old shack with me, but I really think you should go with your family."

Anna listened, but the words didn't make sense. She looked up in confusion? "What?" She glanced at her mama and papa, who were grinning proudly.

"Weren't you listening, child? I said your family is going to Canada, and I wanted to say good-bye, because I really think you should go with them." She was grinning now too, and Anna's head was spinning. She stood to her feet. "We're going where?"

Anna's father crouched in front of her and took his hands in hers. "Mr. and Mrs. Krahn have come back with Mr. Krahn's son and daughter-in-law to oversee this home. They want to buy all our furniture and give us a little bit of money to make up the cost of the boat passage to Canada. With my savings added—the money that couldn't buy us food—we should be able to go very soon."

Anna couldn't see anybody's faces through her watery eyes, and the lump in her throat made it nearly impossible speak, but she wrapped her arms tightly around the old lady beside her.

"There's just one thing I don't understood," Papa said, standing up again. "Mrs. Reimer—I mean Mrs. Krahn," he smiled at the beaming lady, "seems to feel that she is paying back a very great favor, but she won't tell me what it is."

Anna wiped her eyes on the back of her sleeve, and Mama handed her a handkerchief. She blew her nose and told Papa, through chuckles, of the pouch money and the Russian baby pram, and the trip to find the candyman.

Now Papa's eyes filled with tears too. "Well, my dear," he whispered hoarsely, "your obedience to God has earned you this dream." He pulled her into his arms and Mama wrapped her arms around both of them. "Let's go tell the others."

Anna glanced at Mrs. Krahn, who was still sitting on the bed, dabbing her own eyes.

"Go on now," she waved them away. "There will be plenty of time to say good-bye. Unless of course," she added with a teasing smile, "you still don't want to leave."

Anna laughed as they all walked, arm in arm, out to the yard, where Peter chased his brothers and sisters around as though he were ten years old again. Anna pulled free and ran to them.

"We're going to Canada!" she shouted as she broke into their game. Susie and the little ones ran to Anna's side, and she joyfully told them the whole story as they cheered and cried and laughed with her. Only Peter stood silent. When Anna noticed, she looked up to see his eyes filled with tears.

"Papa?" he choked, hanging his head. "I know I've said awful things about your dreams of Canada, and I've acted like I don't need any of you. And I know that I told you I was old enough to live on my own and work for a living, but I missed you all so much. I don't want to be away anymore. Please let me come with you."

So that was it. Papa had sensed that Peter didn't want to go back to the Voth's.

Papa grabbed Peter in the biggest bear hug, and Anna wrapped her arms around them too.

"Of course, you're coming," he cried. "I promised Anna that you would be there, and son, I wouldn't go without you." Then the whole family knelt down in the dry, dusty dirt and said prayers of thanksgiving to the Lord.

"How did you know, Papa?" Anna asked, when they were dusting themselves off. "When you promised that Peter would be coming with us. How did you know?"

"A father knows the heart of his child," Papa answered. "I knew Peter's heart and God knew mine. I just trusted."

Anna cried enough joyful tears that day to drown all the sad ones from the whole last year. It would be weeks before they were ready to leave, but Anna began that night to get ready. There were lots of little things that could wait, like packing her clothes and saying good-bye one more time, but there was one thing that could not wait. Anna found a sharp pencil and borrowed a bit of writing paper from her dear friend, Mrs.Krahn.

"Dearest Johnny," she began. "At last I am coming. . . ."

The Author

Heather Tekavec lives with her husband and three small children in Langley, British Columbia. She is the author of two children's books and writes fiction and devotionals for various magazines for children and teens. This is her first novel.